THE EXPLOSION

Anieza

BIRTH BEGINS WITH DEATH.
OUR LAST DAY IS THE DAWN OF THE FIRST.

- Ozan. The Gift.

UDC 821.161.1
BBK 84(2Ros=Rus)

A64

A64 **Explosion / Anieza. — Gulf Publisher, 2026. — 328 p.**

ISBN: 978-1-918495-80-5 (Paperback)
ISBN: 978-1-918495-81-2 (Hardcover)

What secrets does this book hold? What lies beyond the realm of reality? And most importantly, — will Maryam be able to save her son without becoming a pawn in a game of powerful forces?

This story:

- Keeps you in suspense from the first to the last page.
- Explores the boundaries between reality and fantasy.
- Shows the confrontation between light and darkness through the prism of human destiny.
- Reveals the power of motherly love in the most incredible circumstances.
- Makes you think about the cost of choice.

If you:

- All our lives we have searched for more and craved meaning.
- We felt a craving for light and spiritual development.
- Love exciting stories with unexpected twists.
- Are you interested in mystical mysteries and spiritual searches?
- You admire strong heroes who are able to resist the darkness.

Then this book is for you. Immerse yourself in a world where the line between reality and fantasy blurs, and the fate of the entire world rests on one man. Discover a story that will make your heart beat faster and perhaps even help you find answers to your own questions...

UDC 821.161.1
BBK 84(2Ros=Rus)

18+ Information product sign (Federal Law No. 436-FZ of December 29, 2010)

This book intertwines the truth that the author drew from books: the holy book "Koran", "Ptiha", "Old Testament", "Apocalypse" by Poan the Theologian, "Sufism", "The Power of the Alphabet", as well as the rich imagination of the author and personal experience created this mystical novel "Explosion"

Our entire life is a series of decisions, small, insignificant ones.... Each subsequent decision confronts you with a new choice. Sometimes this choice changes everything, and every minute of your future life depends on it...

(Nicholas Sparks)

There are many plans in a person's heart, but only what the Lord has determined will come to pass.

The Book of Proverbs (Chapter 19, Verse 21)

Table of Contents

Dedication i

Acknowledgements ii

Prologue iii

CHAPTER 1 THE EXPLOSION 1

CHAPTER 2 IN SEARCH OF HER SON 19

CHAPTER 3 LIFE IN THE CITY BEYOND THE WALL 26

CHAPTER 4 LIFE BEYOND THE WALL 34

CHAPTER 5 ARIZAL. THE PATH TO KNOWLEDGE 46

CHAPTER 6 AN UNEXPECTED MEETING 62

CHAPTER 7 THE VESSEL EXPANDS 73

CHAPTER 8 THE STRANGER 83

CHAPTER 9 DOUBTS 98

CHAPTER 10 THE ESCAPE 104

CHAPTER 11 A NEW ACQUAINTANCE 114

CHAPTER 12 HEALING.THE PATH OF THE SUFI 127

CHAPTER 13 THE “BEAST’S” LAIR 142

CHAPTER 14 SHATTERED HOPE 158

CHAPTER 15 THE RESCUE 162

CHAPTER 16 MEETING THE HEAD 190

CHAPTER 17 THE DRAGON 213

CHAPTER 18 REFLECTIONS ON GOOD AND EVIL 229

CHAPTER 19 INITIATION INTO MASTERY 240

CHAPTER 20 THE ESCAPE 252

CHAPTER 21 THE REPENTANCE OF THE FALLEN 272

CHAPTER 22 THE CHOICE 283

EPILOGUE 291

ABOUT THE AUTHOR...294

ANIEZA
EXPLOSION
MYSTICAL ALLEGORICAL NOVEL

Dedication

Dearest reader,

This book is dedicated to you.

To the one who seeks answers and believes in the power of light, even when the world seems shrouded in darkness. To the one who knows that every soul has the capacity to rise— and with its own light, change everything around it.

For me, writing this book was a true miracle. The idea came suddenly—a whole world, alive with characters— and within just two months it took shape, as if this story was eager to be told.

I have poured a piece of my soul into these lines—a faith that love is stronger than fear, and that hope is always alive, only growing stronger in dark times.

May your journey through these pages become a light on a cloudy day, a quiet support when times are hard, and a friend when you feel alone. And if even a single thought from this book resonates in your heart, this story has lived its purpose.

Thank you for being here.

Your heart is a co-author of this story. May the Light hidden within each of us never fade, and always remain a bright beacon.

With love and warmest wishes,

Anieza

Acknowledgements

From the depths of my soul, I thank my beloved husband, who is an inseparable part of my life. His endless patience during the long hours I labored on this book, his steadfast support, and his faith in me were priceless. He shared the joy of creation with me, was my first listener, my wise adviser, and my faithful rock.

I owe special gratitude to my mother, who has stood beside me all her life. Like an invisible umbilical cord, her love and care still bind us, gifting me strength and inspiration. Her presence is an eternal source of warmth and wisdom.

My precious children, my heart is always with you — in every breath, in every line written. You are my greatest happiness and my endless inspiration.

I am infinitely grateful to those who granted me priceless knowledge and opened doors to a world of marvelous discoveries and wonders. Their wisdom and support have been a guiding star on my creative journey.

Prologue

Where the heart weeps, a path opens. Not every darkness comes to destroy. Sometimes it comes to the point of awakening the eyes.

In the beginning, there was Light.

But where there is Light, a shadow always slumbers.

Humanity, having forgotten its origin, approached the brink of oblivion.

And the world shuddered.

The sound of an explosion tore through the fabric of the familiar, and all that seemed eternal turned to dust. Fear spread across the land like cold smoke. And then the children began to vanish. Quietly, without a trace, as if their names were being erased from the book of life. But where the children disappear, God raises mothers.

Maryam remembered all the horror: the black car, the foreign hands that took her son, the scream that did not save—but only pierced the air in helpless anguish.

From that moment, she knew: if there is a road to hell, a mother will walk it barefoot, if only to bring back her child.

And the world responded with a challenge. It is split into two—inside and outside of people.

Light against Darkness. Freedom against the silence of obedience.

A living soul against those who seek to steal its light.

The old was dying, and the new was born in pain. To find her son, she must first find herself, walk the path through the heart of ancient traditions, touch the wisdom of patriarchs in the desert, the revelations of prophets who speak with fire, and the silent grace of those seeking truth.

Maryam stands on the threshold of a new world. The wind whispers ancient names, the night listens without blinking, and the sky waits in silence. She did not choose to be chosen. She is simply a mother. But maternal love is more than a feeling. It is a force that even darkness trembles before.

Maryam has yet to discover who she truly is. But her heart already burns with the Light capable of scattering any darkness.

"God, grant me strength where I am afraid. Grant me Light where Darkness surrounds me. Do not let my heart break—for within it lives the one I am bound to return."

CHAPTER 1
THE EXPLOSION

"Blessed is the one who reads aloud the words of this prophecy, and blessed are those who hear, and who keep what is written in it, for the time is near."

The Revelation of St. John the Divine (Apocalypse), Chapter 1, Verse 3

It happened at dawn, when the world still slumbered in night's embrace. Late autumn cloaked the streets in a delicate veil of snow. The silence was almost tangible—that peculiar pre-dawn stillness when a city hangs suspended between sleep and waking. And then—a blinding flash. It tore the darkness open, and the world shuddered as a dull explosion that ripped the silence apart.

The air trembled. Windows burst with a dry crack, splintering into a thousand shards that cut into living flesh. A shockwave swept through the streets, devouring everything in its path—signs, fences, the fragile remnants of human order.

For a brief moment, everything became light—dazzling, searing, consuming to the bone, as though the earth itself had crumbled into sparks. Time stopped. The world was bleached into silence—shape dissolved, significance erased, leaving only a void. Then came the roar. Heavy, viscous, filling the space between heaven and earth, and it seemed the sky itself was collapsing. For many, that sound was the last they ever heard—their ears, torn by the shockwave, began to bleed, warm trails of red running down their cheeks. Those who managed to tear themselves from the arms of sleep awoke to unspeakable horror. The light faded. In its place came a gray veil—a mixture of snow and ash settling over lifeless human faces. No one wept. Not yet.

Emotions would come later, when the mind caught up with the horror. And now, instead of nerves, there was only a tight, numb knot — as if their minds refused to accept the reality unfolding before them.

The cold cut to the bone. First arrived the hulking buses, their weight pressing into the street as they moved with deliberate slowness.

Their doors hissed open, and from within emerged people in protective gear — thick jackets, gloves, masks covering the lower half of their faces.

They began their work immediately — without a word, without haste. Some examined those lying on the ground, carefully checking for a pulse. Others helped those still able to walk, supporting them by the arms. Still others, with astonishing precision, placed the wounded onto stretchers and carried them into the buses. Their movements were precise, efficient. No panic. No confusion. Only a cold, methodical focus.

When the first buses, now full, began to pull away slowly, new vehicles emerged from the veil of smoke. Black. Unmarked. They moved almost silently, and the people inside — dressed in identical dark coats and thick masks — looked like ghosts.

These did not tend to the wounded. They moved with purpose, scanning the crowd and seeking out young boys, girls, and teenagers. Without explanation, without a single word, they approached, took the young ones by the hand, and led them toward the waiting vehicles. If anyone resisted, the response was soft yet unyielding — any attempt to break free was swiftly and firmly subdued. Everything happened quickly, almost mechanically, as if following a prewritten algorithm.

When she returned to her senses, the first thing she saw through the haze and chaos was her fifteen-year-old son. He was being led toward one of the black vans. He kept looking back, searching for her with desperate eyes — but between them already stood a wall of unfamiliar backs. She lunged forward, stumbling over debris, falling, rising again.

The snow beneath her feet had turned into filthy slush, but she felt neither the cold nor the pain — only the frantic pounding of her heart, beating out a single rhythm: "My son. My son. My son." With a hoarse cry, she threw herself into the group surrounding her child.

Her trembling hands clutched wildly — a sleeve, a shoulder, any scrap of fabric she could seize. She fought like a bird caught in a snare, pushing, tearing, forcing her way toward him.

"Let him go! He's just a child!" Her voice cracked, breaking into a ragged whisper, then rose again into a scream:

"He's my son! You can't take him!"

Her face had gone ashen with terror, but her eyes blazed with such intensity it seemed they could burn through armor. In that moment, for her, there was only one person in the world — her son.

"Stop! What are you doing? Where are you taking him?" She screamed, clutching at the sleeve of a tall man in a black jacket marked with an insignia on the arm. He didn't even turn his head.

"To the same place they're taking everyone else," came the indifferent reply. And that was all. No word for the mother who had carried, raised, and loved her child.

Nothing.

She lunged toward the vehicle, grabbing the door handle — her last desperate attempt to hold on to her son.

"Then take me too!" she begged. "No. You can't go there." "Please... at least tell me where I can find him."

It was the final stage of despair — when strength has already left you, when you understand there is no changing what's been set in motion. All that remains is to plead humbly, clinging to even the faintest chance of keeping a connection with the one being torn from you.

One of them, who seemed older than the rest, stopped and glanced at her. His eyes showed no kindness, just a tired, blank coldness. The car doors slammed shut. Engines roared to life, and the black convoy began to move, carrying her son away along with the other children.

The grief-stricken mothers stood motionless on the road, their bodies seemingly rooted to the ashen earth. They were afraid to move, afraid to blink, afraid to look away from the retreating black dots of the departing vehicles. It felt as though if they did — if they broke that gaze — the fragile thread connecting them to their children would snap forever.

The dots disappeared, and sadness rushed over them like a storm. Pain should have an end, a point where the heart can't take anymore. But still, it kept beating, stubborn and unwilling to give in to loss.

Why hadn't it stopped when that last black speck disappeared? "No... this can't happen. This isn't the end. He's alive — and I will find him." "Calm down. Think. Where could they have taken him? It must be connected to the upper ranks. They've been planning something for a long time... everyone felt it, but no one imagined it would happen so soon." Swaying unsteadily, she began to walk in the direction the convoy had gone. Her head throbbed; a dull roar filled her ears. Around her stretched blackened, scorched fields dusted with white ash, and everywhere she looked, bodies... bodies... bodies.

The survivors were slowly regaining their senses. Consciousness returned hand in hand with a primal, animal fear. People wandered like shadows, aimless, not knowing where to go or what to do next. The horror of what they had lived through was etched in their eyes. Night passed unnoticed. Her strength was fading, and by midnight she stumbled upon a half-ruined house. Inside, the air was damp and thick with smoke. She curled up in a corner, hugging her knees, and tried to fall asleep. Her sleep was uneasy—haunted by screams, blasts, and cries. A soft rustling sound jolted her awake.

Something moved in the darkness, accompanied by a soft whimper. Fighting the rising fear, she slowly got to her feet and stepped closer. Amid a heap of rubble — torn rags, splintered wood, and shattered glass, sat a little girl. Frightened, frail, her enormous eyes reflected a world that had collapsed overnight. She was no more than five years old. Maryam's heart clenched. Moving slowly, careful not to scare the child further, she knelt beside her and gently touched her shoulder. The girl flinched and shrank back, but Maryam didn't withdraw. She stretched out her arms and softly called:

"What is your name?" No answer — only the trembling of tiny shoulders.

"My name is Maryam," she continued, her voice a soft caress. "I will not hurt you. I will just sit beside you. I'm scared too... I lost my son." The child quieted. A fragile glimmer of trust flickered in her wide eyes.

Maryam called out once more, and this time the girl leaned closer to her.

She pressed her small body against the woman, without a single tear — only quiet, shuddering tremors. It was a silent cry.

"Where are your parents?" Maryam asked softly, stroking the child's tangled hair.

The girl did not answer. Only her uneven breathing revealed the tragedy hidden inside.

Perhaps the explosion and the terror she endured took away her speech. I hope it's only temporary, Maryam thought, rocking her gently until she fell asleep. She carefully laid the child down on a pile of rags and covered her with something resembling a blanket. The night grew colder.

I need to sleep, or tomorrow I won't have the strength for the road. What should I do? Where should I go? I'll think about it tomorrow. For now — sleep.

At dawn, she was awakened by a soft, plaintive whimper. The little girl sat beside her, tugging at the hem of her shirt.

Hungry, Maryam thought as she rose. I have to find something—anything—to eat.

In the gray morning light, the destruction became unmistakably clear. The kitchen had taken the worst of the blast. Part of the roof had collapsed, and during the night, snow had drifted inside. It lay over the soot like a thin shroud, covering every surface in a cold, fragile white.

The table still stood in the center of the room—or rather, what was left of it: a charred frame, blackened legs. The cabinets hung crooked. Glass crunched beneath her feet. Torn sacks of grain were scattered across the floor, their contents mixed with ash and splinters.

She picked up a packet of biscuits. The paper fell apart in her hands. Inside was nothing but gray dust, bitter with the smell of smoke. A few cans lay against the wall. With a flicker of hope, she lifted one—but the lid had swollen, and a cloudy liquid seeped from the seams. It was inedible.

Ash coated everything—the furniture, the floor, her own hands. Her mouth was so dry it hurt to swallow. She ran her tongue over her cracked lips.

Water. At least water.

Carefully stepping over the debris, she noticed a small box of matches among the scattered cutlery. She picked it up and shook it gently. Several matches rattled inside.

"Lucky," she whispered.

Outside, snow covered the ruins, settling over blackened beams and broken walls, softening the harsh outlines of destruction. The world seemed unnaturally still.

She gathered splintered boards and broken chair legs and built a fire. The first match died in the wind. The second caught—the flame trembled, hissed, then slowly steadied.

In the rubble, she found a blackened pot. She filled it with the cleanest layer of snow and set it over the fire. The flames swayed in the wind; smoke stung her eyes. The snow melted slowly, shrinking into cloudy water. From a full pot, she got barely a cup and a half.

She repeated the process again and again until, at last, she had a whole pot—murky, with a faint chemical tang, but thoroughly boiled.

There was no way of knowing what kind of explosion it had been, or what was settling onto the earth with the snow.

But there was no choice.

She tasted it first. Waited.

Her throat did not tighten. No nausea came.

Only then did she carry the water inside.

The little girl sat on the floor with her knees drawn to her chest. When Maryam handed her the cup, the child seized it with both hands and drank quickly, in small, desperate gulps, as if afraid it might be taken away.

It did not ease the hunger, but it brought brief relief.

The girl grew quiet, watching Maryam with a seriousness far beyond her years. Maryam sat beside her, heavy thoughts pressing in.

Will she survive the road?

Where is my son?

Is he alive?

Outside, the wind began to howl.

Maryam stood.

"Stay here," she said softly, and stepped into the yard.

A small dog stood near the ruins—thin, its fur matted with dirt. It wagged its tail cautiously, as though grateful to see a human face.

The thought came instantly.

Lord, forgive me... but we have no choice. This is no time for sentiment.

Maryam crouched and extended her hand.

The dog ran to her trustingly and pressed its wet nose into her palm.

Her heart tightened painfully.

Her hand did not tremble.

When the animal turned its head, she struck it with a stone. It shuddered once and fell still.

"Thank God... I didn't have to strike twice," she whispered, nausea rising in her throat.

She carried the body behind the house and prepared it quickly — the child mustn't see.

Her emotions locked themselves deep inside; her nerves stretched to their limit.

She was no longer simply a woman.

She was a mother, ready to do anything to save her son.

When Maryam returned to the house with the meat, she met the girl's questioning gaze.

"A rabbit ran by," she said quietly in answer to the silent question. "An old one. It wouldn't have survived anyway… And you know, I think it chose to help us."

The girl looked at her for a long time. The thought seemed to calm her; she gave a faint nod.

"Don't be sad. Go see if you can find some salt — otherwise the soup will taste awful."

The child brightened, jumped up, and ran off to look for it.

Thank God — at least it will distract her from dark thoughts, Maryam thought.

Within five minutes, the girl was tugging at her dress, holding out a salt shaker.

"What a clever girl you are! Now we'll have real soup," Maryam said with a smile. "Come on — let's gather more wood."

She lifted the child into her arms and went outside. There was enough broken furniture to build several more fires. They filled the pot with snow again and set it over their makeshift hearth. Soon, the water boiled.

Maryam lowered the meat into it and dragged an old sofa closer to the fire.

The girl pressed against her and grew still, mesmerized by the tongues of flame. Maryam gently stroked her head, feeling the child slowly begin to relax.

"Our soup is ready."

She poured it into cups that had miraculously survived in the kitchen. They ate silently, without haste.

By the fire, the heaviest burdens fade. Fire purifies.

“Thank God for everything,” Maryam said as she rose. They could not sit long. The road ahead meant uncertainty.

She looked thoughtfully at the quiet child beside her.

What am I going to do with you?

As if sensing her doubt, the little girl whimpered softly.

“Don’t cry,” Maryam whispered, drawing her close. “I won’t leave you alone. You’re coming with me.”

The girl sniffed and searched her face intently, as though trying to decide whether she could trust her.

Day was steadily taking hold. Slanting rays of sunlight streamed through the empty window frames, falling in pale bands across the dust-covered floor.

Maryam drew a deep breath and looked around the house again, this time without panic. It was impossible to live here. The smell of smoke still lingered; the beams were blackened in places and cracked sharply in the frost. The house was standing — but only as if by sheer stubbornness.

The frost will only grow harsher. I need to find warm clothes and get out of here, she thought, moving through the surviving rooms until she came upon a child’s bedroom.

Here, the destruction seemed gentler. The walls had held, but the windows were shattered; toys lay scattered across the floor, a small chair overturned. An open book rested where it had fallen, lightly dusted with ash. She turned her gaze away and forced herself to focus.

Among the belongings she found was a child's jacket, a hat, and sturdy shoes.

Good… Now mittens would be perfect…

They were in the pocket.

Thank God.

As she stepped into the adjoining room, a thought flickered through her mind: Where is this girl's family?

In the ruins, she found a nursery. Time seemed to have frozen at the moment of the catastrophe—scattered toys, a toppled little chair, an open picture book on the floor... She pressed a hand to her mouth, fighting back tears, then forced herself to focus.

Among the debris, she found a jacket, boots, and a wool hat.

If only I could find mittens, she thought—and as if in answer, there they were, tucked into the jacket pocket.

Where is the family that lived here? Maryam wondered, gripping the clothes.

In the next room, her gaze fell on a scarf and a heavy autumn coat. It would not truly warm her, but there was no choice. Beggars can't be choosers, she thought, pulling on the coat and wrapping the scarf over her head. That was better.

Warmth began to spread through her battered body. For a moment, she wanted nothing more than to close her eyes and sleep. Hot food and dry clothes had done their work.

No... don't relax. Your son. Stop. Be strong.

In the corridor, she noticed a staircase leading down. Carefully, she descended, trying not to catch the unstable banister. Hardly any light reached that far; she didn't see the obstacle until she stumbled over something solid and nearly fell.

Looking closer, she made out the shape of a human body. The man lay face down. Maryam turned him over slowly—a horrific wound gaped on his forehead, and terror was frozen in his glassy eyes.

That must be the girl's father.

Her chest tightened. She swallowed, trying to stop the trembling in her fingers, and gently closed his eyes.

The child mustn't see him like this, she told herself, and rose. Her legs felt weak; a dull ringing filled her ears. Maryam rested her forehead against the cold wall and took several slow breaths.

Calm down. Hold it together.

She straightened, wiped her face, and went through the rooms gathering any warm clothes that might be useful on the road ahead.

Then she froze.

Maryam's heart thudded. She stepped carefully over shattered wood and dust, her breath shallow in the stale air. Another low sound came from the figure on the floor—a moan, a whimper; she couldn't tell.

The woman's face was half-hidden in shadow, her hair fallen across her cheek, but her eyes fluttered open as Maryam approached—full of pain and confusion.

Her face was coated in dust; her lips were cracked and dry. The collapse of the roof must have trapped her; she had lost consciousness. Maryam shifted the debris aside and carefully pulled her free. The woman was pale and disoriented, her gaze unfocused.

Most likely a concussion... and possibly a broken arm. Thank God—the girl's mother is alive. That makes things a little easier, Maryam thought.

The woman blinked at her, voice rough and trembling.

"Who are you? Where is my daughter? My husband? What happened?"

The questions spilled out in a hoarse rush.

"Calm down," Maryam said softly. "Your daughter is safe."

"And my husband...?"

Maryam hesitated, searching for words. To tell the truth now would be to strip the woman of her last support.

"We'll find him," she said at last, looking straight into her eyes. "Right now, what matters is taking care of you and your daughter."

The woman tried to stand, but her legs gave way; she nearly fell. Maryam caught her in time, steadying her by the elbow.

"Easy. Save your strength. Your daughter needs you. What is your name?"

"Anna," she whispered after a pause. "And yours?"

"Maryam," she replied. "Wait here—I'll bring your daughter."

She went back to the kitchen.

The little girl looked up, then sprang to her feet and rushed into Maryam's arms, clinging to her neck as tears slipped silently down her cheeks.

Hush now, don't cry," Maryam soothed. "I found your mother."

Terror and joy crossed the child's face at once.

"Don't worry. She's alive."

The girl slipped from her embrace and tugged impatiently at Maryam's sleeve.

"Don't rush. Your mother is very tired. Here—take this blanket, and I'll bring the rest of our soup and some hot water. She needs strength."

The girl nodded gratefully, helped gather what little they had, and then—barefoot, trembling with excitement—pulled Maryam towards the room. Anna sat as before, eyes closed.

When the girl saw her mother, she flung herself into her arms. Anna shuddered, opened her eyes, and clutched the child tightly, caressing her as tears ran down her face. Their tears met and merged, washing away fear and horror.

Maryam did not try to comfort them. They needed this moment—they needed to let the terror of that morning pour out.

When the tears finally stopped, the little girl fell asleep, her face buried against her mother's chest. Anna looked at her with boundless love.

“What’s her name?” Maryam asked softly.

“Yulia,” Anna answered.

“Yulia,” Maryam repeated. “A beautiful name. Lay her on the bed and eat something.”

Anna didn’t want to let go of the child she had just regained, but she knew Maryam was right—her strength was failing. With a heavy heart, she handed the girl to Maryam. Her arm throbbed, and hunger made itself known.

Maryam tore a sheet into strips and bound the arm tightly. The fracture seemed clean—no displacement. Once she had studied at a medical university and still remembered a little anatomy. She never became a doctor; that demanded a certain temperament, and she had been too sensitive...

But now all sentimentality had vanished without a trace. All that remained was a heart armoured in pain—a mother’s heart, burning with the need to find her son.

Maryam took a small pot and fed the exhausted woman. When Anna had eaten, she sank into a deep sleep.

Maryam covered mother and child with a blanket and stepped out, thinking they couldn’t stay long—looters could appear at any moment.

She packed the essentials into a bag, added the scraps of food she had found in the house, and sat down to collect her thoughts.

She had to weigh everything.

Where should we go? Anna is still weak; we’ll have to stay here another day. One more day. And my son... what is happening to him now? What suffering is he enduring?

Stop. Enough. If I let these thoughts consume me, they'll destroy me. I must stay strong. He needs me.

Wrapping herself in a blanket, she fell into a restless, vigilant sleep. Outside, dawn slowly turned the sky grey. The world woke in silence—no birdsong, no whisper of wind.

Maryam opened her eyes, stood, and gently woke Anna and Yulia.

"Wake up. We can't stay here. It's dangerous."

Anna startled, opened her eyes, and stared for a few seconds without understanding. Then she tried to stand—and, to Maryam's relief, she managed it. Maryam exhaled, grateful—thank God—and for the first time in a long while she smiled.

"Anna," she asked suddenly, "do you believe in God?"

"Yes," Anna said.

"Then let's pray. Since the explosion, I haven't prayed once."

They knelt. Their whispers blended together, and Yulia's small, uneven voice gave the prayer a special purity and calm. The anxiety that had gripped them for so long began to loosen, giving way to a faint sense of peace.

In a lighter mood, they began to prepare for the road ahead. In the kitchen, behind a cabinet, Anna found a real treasure—tea and coffee, miraculously spared. And little Yulia, glowing with joy, brought over her backpack and proudly produced a packet of biscuits. A feast, in the midst of ruin.

Thanking God for these finds, they packed for the journey: three bottles of water, what food remained, the warm clothes they had gathered—everything divided carefully between their backpacks.

Maryam checked the bandage on Anna's arm. The injury wasn't serious, but it needed care.

That was it.

They looked at one another, sat for a moment, then stood and stepped over the threshold of the house.

CHAPTER 2
IN SEARCH OF HER SON

A biting cold met them the moment they stepped outside. At least there was no wind — that was something to be grateful for before them stretched a scene that stole their breath away. An apocalypse in all its bleakness: shattered houses, charred trees, and everywhere — lifeless bodies of people and animals. Some lay curled up, others sprawled with arms outstretched, as if trying to embrace the earth in their final moment. Maryam tried not to look, but her eyes kept catching on the details — a child's sandal, a scorched handbag, a broken doll...

The world dissolved into a palette of black and gray. The explosion had stirred the air into chaos. At first, a hurricane-force wind swept everything it could carry away from the city, fragments of light buildings, people, and even stones. Then, as if guided by some unseen will, the wind suddenly reversed, surging back toward the city from all sides at once. Many who had survived the initial blast perished in the roaring, fire-breathing inferno that followed.

They walked in silence, forcing themselves not to linger on the horror around them.

Then — a sound.

Vehicles were approaching fast.

"Get down," Maryam whispered, dropping to the cold ground strewn with ash and shards. All three flattened themselves among the ruins, pressing their bodies to the earth, pretending to be dead.

The vehicles thundered past, engines roaring, kicking clouds of dust into the air.

When the noise faded, Maryam cautiously raised her head. Her throat burned from the dust; a sharp ringing filled her ears.

“Where are they going?” Yulia whispered.

“I don’t know...” Maryam replied, watching them disappear into the distance. The dust slowly settled, revealing the empty road once more. “Maybe we should go that way too. We’ll figure out later who can be trusted.”

They stood up, looked at one another, and suddenly burst out laughing. A layer of white ash coated their faces, turning them into almost theatrical masks. The laughter eased the tension, if only for a moment.

Maryam watched Yulia fool around and thought about how different children were from adults. Somehow, inexplicably, they knew how to find joy even amid chaos and destruction.

Brushing the ash from themselves, they moved on.

Before long, people appeared ahead. The same vehicles that had sped past them earlier were now parked there. Figures in protective suits and masks bustled about, gathering survivors — some walking on their own, others carried on makeshift stretchers.

Maryam approached the driver of one of the trucks. He sat in the cab, dark glasses still on, scribbling something in a notebook.

“Where are you taking them?” she asked, striving to keep her voice calm.

The man looked up. His face was tired and ashen, deep wrinkles etched around his eyes.

"Out of the city," he said. "They've already built a wall there and are constructing a new city. This one will be sealed off soon. Anyone who stays behind won't be allowed through the gates. There will be a thorough screening."

"What kind of screening?" Maryam asked.

"Radiation," he replied grimly. "You see, it wasn't just an explosion. That white ash everywhere — it's radiation. And it mutates. We don't fully understand it yet, but we know one thing: people become extremely aggressive. They stop being human — just wild beasts with red eyes. I've seen it myself. It's terrifying."

The women exchanged frightened glances. Anna instinctively pulled Yulia close. The girl fell silent, clutching her mother's hand.

"Fortunately, it doesn't affect everyone," the man continued. "We still don't know why. There's a lot to do — gather the survivors and take them first into isolation. After a thorough check, if everything is fine, they'll be sent to the new city. Construction is nearly complete. You should come with us. You won't survive on your own."

Maryam looked at Anna, then at Yulia.

The girl stared at her with wide eyes and suddenly asked,

"Aunt Maryam... will we find Daddy?"

Maryam swallowed the lump in her throat. She didn't promise. She didn't lie.

"We'll keep looking," she said softly.

"Tell me... maybe you know," she turned to the driver again.

"Where are the teenagers taken?"

The man met her question with a heavy, piercing gaze.

"Why do you want to know?"

"My son is there," she whispered. Unbearable pain flickered in her eyes.

He fell silent, as if weighing something. His fingers tightened around the steering wheel, his gaze drifting beyond the line of ruined houses.

"Don't look for him," he said at last, quietly, almost in a whisper. "It's useless."

"Please..." Maryam stepped closer and touched his arm. "Tell me something. Anything. Where can I find him?"

The man sighed heavily, his shoulders slumping.

"Listen. I understand your pain, but I can't help you. We're all just trying to survive, and we're forbidden to talk about this. But..." He hesitated, then continued, as if having made a decision. "There are rumors. They say younger teenagers are sent to closed camps. They're creating a special army there — no room for pity or compassion. People like... robots."

The ground seemed to vanish beneath Maryam's feet.

"Camps? Where are they?"

"On the far side of the city, away from the center. But getting there isn't easy. It's like a separate state, with its own laws. You can't slip in unnoticed. If you decide to go, be very careful."

"Can you take a woman with a child?" Maryam asked, pointing to Anna and Yulia.

"Yes," he said. "We're taking everyone beyond the Wall."

"And you?" Anna exclaimed.

"Me?" Maryam shook her head. "I can't go with you. I have to find my son."

She helped Anna and Yulia climb into the truck and stood for a long time on the road, watching the vehicles disappear.

An oppressive silence settled in.

Her thoughts swarmed like insects. While she had been caring for Anna and Yulia, there had been no time to think. Now, there was too much of it. A mother's imagination shows no mercy. When your child is far away and there is no contact, the mind paints the most terrifying images.

Stop. They won't kill them.

She knew that already.

But what will they do to them? How will they corrupt their minds?

That was what truly terrified her.

"Lord..." she prayed silently. "Lord, save my son and all the children. I beg You — do not let them perish, neither in body nor in soul."

She had taught her son to pray since early childhood. But would he remember prayer now, wherever he was?

"Lord, give him strength," the desperate mother whispered, staring into the gray sky.

Her heart clenched with loneliness and despair. The world had turned into a nightmare in which she was nothing more than a silent witness.

In the distance, new sounds arose. Groups of people were approaching — those who hadn't found space in the trucks, still searching for a way to escape the doomed city. Hungry, exhausted, sorrow in every pair of eyes. A long journey lay ahead, and their supplies were already running out.

They passed by.

Gathering her remaining strength, Maryam headed in the direction the driver had indicated. Somewhere out there, perhaps, were the camps for young soldiers.

She was terribly tired, and hunger gnawed at her. From her meager supplies, only a few cookies and a small pouch of rusks remained.

Maryam smiled faintly, remembering the words of her newfound friend:

"These rusks were once given to me by a monk. They may come in handy one day."

Anna had hugged her goodbye and slipped the pouch into her pocket.

Yes, they truly will, Maryam thought now.

She took out the pouch and read the faded inscription:

"Rusks from Saint Seraphim of Sarov."

Scooping a small handful, she sighed and trudged on.

Lord... how many mothers like me are there — left without their sons?

The explosion was not the worst of it. Ahead lay radiation and hunger. The land had been scorched as if by fire. Almost everything was dead, and the supplies people still had would soon be gone.

What happens next?

How does one go on living?

CHAPTER 3

LIFE IN THE CITY BEYOND THE WALL

The far end of the city was alive with frantic activity.

Medics in radiation suits hurried through the ruins, shouting to one another, hauling stretchers, issuing sharp commands. There was far more work than they could possibly manage. People lay everywhere—some unconscious, some groaning in pain, and some who would never open their eyes again.

It was a sight that froze the blood.

Looking at it, Maryam understood that the world she had known was gone forever.

She stopped near a group of doctors lifting a woman onto a stretcher.

“What’s wrong with her?” Maryam asked.

“Radiation,” one of the medics replied curtly, without lifting his head.

“Be careful,” another added. “If you see people with red eyes—run. They’re extremely aggressive. Don’t touch them.” He studied Maryam more closely. “How long have you been here? You need to be examined.”

Maryam explained that she had arrived only recently and, aside from hunger, felt no alarming symptoms. The doctor examined her carefully.

"Thank God—you're healthy," he said at last. "This infection spreads through the air. Avoiding exposure is almost impossible. It's spreading fast."

Nearby, residents without protective suits watched in fear, uncertain of what awaited them. Horror and utter hopelessness filled their eyes—the dreadful thought that they might be next.

In the square, cages had been set up.

Inside them were the infected.

Their eyes were bloodshot; their gazes filled with madness. Little remained of what had once been human. They hurled themselves against the bars with savage fury, like wild animals.

It was terrifying.

Maryam turned away. Pain and fear were everywhere. Hunger and loss had taken their toll.

She remembered the rusks Anna had given her and ate a few.

I need to find food, she thought, heading toward an abandoned shop, hoping that the old shelves might still hold something edible.

Her head spun from hunger, and thirst burned her throat.

Near the shop, she noticed several men in protective suits gesturing toward something inside the darkened interior. Her heart began to race as she approached the window.

What she saw stunned her.

Canned goods still lined the shelves. Bottles of water. Boxes of cookies—and more.

How is there still so much food here? She wondered, momentarily forgetting her fear of radiation.

She was about to rush inside when approaching footsteps stopped her.

One of the suited men dropped to his knees and began sweeping everything off the shelves.

Suddenly, his hand froze.

"I found it! Hurry!" he shouted.

The others rushed toward him.

Fearing discovery, Maryam slipped back into the shadows. She knew she had to act immediately—before anyone noticed her.

She darted into the shop.

There was no time to think. She grabbed what mattered most—bottled water and canned food. Radiation couldn't penetrate sealed metal, and the risk of contamination was lower.

She stuffed several cans into her backpack.

At that moment, the door creaked open.

A man with red eyes stepped inside.

His movements were erratic, uncoordinated—he was clearly not in his right mind.

Maryam froze, afraid even to breathe.

Then his gaze locked onto her.

He turned and began moving toward her.

Lord, no... she prayed silently, snatching a bottle of water as she bolted for the exit.

He lunged after her.

Their strength was unequal. His aggression drove him with animal force, and he was nearly catching up. But his movements were chaotic—he couldn't run straight, veering wildly from side to side. That slowed him just enough.

Maryam reached a high wall and spotted a door.

She burst inside.

People rushed toward her and slammed the door shut, throwing a heavy bolt across it.

"How did you get in here?" a young woman in a radiation suit demanded. "The door was locked!"

"No," Maryam gasped. "A strange man was chasing me. The door was open—I ran inside."

"Did he touch you?" the woman asked sharply, watching her closely.

"No. He didn't have time."

"That's good," another medic said automatically. "Otherwise, you'd infect everyone here."

"I'm fine," Maryam insisted. "I just arrived. I haven't had contact with anyone."

They called others over and examined her carefully. Pupils normal. Eyes clear. Pulse elevated—but only from running.

“All right,” they said at last. “You’re clear. You may go. Someone will show you around.”

Maryam stepped outside.

The same bleak landscape unfolded before her—a reality that had already begun to feel disturbingly familiar.

After the explosion, the city had been rebuilt with astonishing speed.

The weapon that had been used was unlike anything before. It had not destroyed the earth itself—there was no need. Radiation had spread only twenty to thirty centimeters above the surface. Everything higher had either perished or been irreversibly damaged. Those who had fallen to the ground in time, who had managed to dig in even slightly, had a chance to survive.

Mother Earth had saved them.

Taking this into account, people had built dugout homes. Pits were carved directly into the ground and turned into small dwellings. The interiors were finished with clay; after whitewashing, they became unexpectedly warm and natural. Above, mesh, branches, moss, and soil were layered over the roofs. Once the grass grew, the houses would be nearly invisible.

Inside, stoves were installed, with chimneys designed so that—if God forbid another explosion occurred—the flue could be sealed shut. In such shelters, the new weapon could not penetrate.

People had a chance.

The speed of construction was astonishing. People worked tirelessly, like ants. It was as if the local authorities had foreseen this catastrophe and prepared in advance.

Maryam's thoughts were interrupted when a young man gently tugged at her sleeve.

"Come with me," he said. "I'll take you to the others."

She followed him, unable to stop marveling at the order around her. Everything functioned with remarkable precision, as if everyone already knew exactly what to do.

How did they manage all this so quickly? she wondered.

About a hundred meters ahead stood a two-story building—strikingly different from the surrounding dugouts.

I wonder what's inside.

The young man left her among the other survivors and walked away.

Attempts at conversation led nowhere. Faces were rigid, eyes dull. Heavy, grim thoughts consumed them—and no wonder. They had lost everything: loved ones, homes, their former lives. Their familiar world had collapsed in an instant, leaving only pain and fear behind.

Maryam approached a woman sitting in a corner. She was softly humming, tears streaming down her face.

She looks so much like Anna, Maryam thought. The same inner strength, despite everything.

The woman introduced herself as Alexandra.

Her story was no less tragic. At the moment of the explosion, she had been visiting a friend. At home were her husband, a nanny, and her two children.

"My daughter just turned twelve," Alexandra said quietly. "My son is five. I don't know what happened to them."

"Thinking about it is unbearable," she added, "yet I still hope to find them here. I pray for them day and night."

When Alexandra fell silent, Maryam drew a deep breath and, in the same hushed tone, shared her own story—about her son, about the search, about the suffocating weight of not knowing.

Alexandra listened without interrupting. Compassion filled her eyes.

"I haven't heard anything about the teenagers," she said softly at last. "But I'll try to find out. There's a young medic here—we've become friendly. He's very resourceful. Knows everything about everyone."

They agreed to meet the next day.

But that meeting was never meant to happen.

Suddenly, an unfamiliar man approached Maryam.

"Please come with me," he said calmly, without preamble.

Maryam rose without a word. Questions hovered on her lips, but something in his presence compelled obedience.

They were heading toward the same two-story building that stood apart from the surrounding dugouts.

Anxiety tightened her chest.

Where is he taking me? Will I learn anything about my son? How weary my heart is... Lord, help him. Give him strength.

They stopped at a heavy door.

The man motioned for her to enter, switched on a lamp, and led her down a staircase.

She was struck at once—the stairs were solidly built: wide, even steps, sturdy railings, smooth walls. Everything here felt strong and reliable.

Who built this? And why such solidity?

At the bottom, a long corridor stretched before them, bathed in soft white light. At its far end stood a massive metal door fitted with a complex, high-tech locking system and heavy bolts.

Thick steel plates, coated with a special anti-corrosion compound, formed what looked like an impenetrable barrier. Along the perimeter ran powerful pneumatic seals—designed to withstand even another explosion.

The man entered a code.

With a muted hiss, the door slid open.

Beyond it lay a spacious hall—not merely a shelter, but a first-class bunker.

The walls were faced with light-colored stone; the ceiling was fitted with discreet lighting that cast a clean, even glow. There was no trace of soot or smoke—only calm, controlled illumination. The floor was laid with solid tiles, and along the perimeter stood comfortable sofas and armchairs, with low wooden tables placed between them.

Every detail spoke of careful planning and deliberate foresight.

The contrast between the rough simplicity of the dugouts above and the refined interior of the bunker was striking.

"Excuse me," Maryam said at last, unable to hide her surprise. "Is this bunker only for the chosen few?"

The man smiled faintly, just at the corner of his mouth.

"No," he replied. "Even if we had to shelter every resident of the city, there would be enough space for everyone. There are two more fully equipped levels below—kitchens, a medical unit, and all necessary facilities. We prepared well."

They stopped in front of another door.

The man knocked. The sound echoed deeply through the vault-like space.

"Come in," came a voice—authoritative, yet calm and steady.

The guide stepped aside.

"Don't be afraid," he said quietly. "Everything is fine. Go ahead."

Maryam took a breath and stepped inside.

CHAPTER 4
LIFE BEYOND THE WALL

MIKHAIL.

The moment she crossed the threshold, she froze in astonishment.

Everything about it suggested this was no hiding place, but a place where destinies were decided.

The room she entered seemed to transport her into another world—one she had believed lost forever.

The elegant interior struck her with its careful design. From the outside, the structure appeared modest, almost crude. Inside, it was astonishingly solid. Every detail seemed to have been meticulously planned long before the catastrophe.

A large decorative window was framed by heavy yet graceful curtains. A powerful ventilation system with advanced filters filled the room with clean air, a luxury the rest of the city could only dream of. In one corner stood a magnificent antique bookcase filled with books. A soft carpet covered the floor. At the center of the room stood a carved desk with a computer.

And—miracle of miracles—it was working.

There was no electricity anywhere in the city, let alone internet. Yet here, all of it existed.

How is this possible? she wondered.

Behind the desk sat a man in his early fifties. Noble gray streaks softened his dark complexion. His attentive eyes held more than intelligence—there was strength in them, a disciplined coldness, and something else, elusive, that sent a chill down Maryam's spine.

He studied her closely, almost analytically, as if trying to read thoughts buried deep within her.

"What is your name?" he asked quietly.

"Maryam," she replied.

"Where are you from?"

"From the city. When the explosion happened..." Her voice trembled. "My son was taken. I'm looking for him. Can you help me?"

He paused before answering.

"Yes. It's possible I can help you. But first, you need to eat and rest. I believe you are very tired."

"Thank you. I am. But more in spirit than in body. I'm worn down by worry for my son."

He inclined his head.

"Do not worry. As far as I know, your son is alive. You have no reason to fear."

"But I need to see him. I must know he's all right. Until then, I can't even breathe properly. I need to see my son."

"I understand. But first—you must rest."

He pressed a button on the desk. The door opened, and the same guide appeared.

“Please escort the lady to the Blue Room.”

A sense of unease crept over Maryam. Something in this man’s gaze unsettled her, as though he already knew far more about her than he should. Her fingers curled involuntarily as she tried to steady the trembling inside her.

Who is he?

What did he want?

How can he speak of my son with such certainty?

But her strength was failing. Her legs felt weak with exhaustion, and a dull pressure pulsed at her temples. Clenching her fists, she followed the guide.

The corridor was nearly silent. They ascended a spiral staircase to the upper floor.

The room she was led into was bright and unexpectedly cozy, with a small window draped in curtains. She had imagined a windowless dugout, but this felt almost like home.

A bed stood against the wall, and at the sight of it, she longed to sink into its soft sheets. Nearby was an armchair and a writing desk. Beyond them—a door to the bathroom.

A bath...

The mere thought of warm water made her muscles seize.

Three weeks of endless travel, hunger, thirst, fear—every muscle, every joint bore the memory of it. And here—everything was abundant. Cleanliness. Warmth. Calm.

Why?

What do they want from me?

Her son? He had already been taken. What else was left?

Nothing but her soul.

But they can't take that... can they?

Although... who knows.

All right, she decided. I'll accept part of their kindness for now. We'll see.

That was one of her husband's favorite phrases, and it had always made her smile.

Where is he now?

Her thoughts returned to that morning—when men in uniform burst into their home without warning and took her husband away. Endless interrogations followed. Searches. Long evenings with lawyers and officials. They had never managed to formally accuse him. Their accounts were frozen.

And then the explosion happened.

Whether he was alive, she didn't know.

Her only goal now was to find and save her son. After that—God willing—they would all be reunited.

"Lord, help us,"— she whispered.

Maryam undressed slowly and entered the bathroom. A marble countertop veined with blue, wooden floors, and pale blue silk wallpaper created a soothing harmony. She filled the tub and slipped into the water.

For the first time in a long while, she allowed herself to relax.

Warmth enveloped her. Her eyelids grew heavy...

A loud knock at the door jolted her upright—the water was already brushing her nose.

“Whew... another moment and I might have drowned.”

Oh God. I must be careful. I have to think of my son.

She jumped out of the tub, wrapped herself in a soft robe, and opened the door slightly, still wiping water from her face.

The same man stood there.

As if he had been waiting.

Or watching.

“I brought you food,” he said, handing her a tray. “Rest is important. But... be careful. It would be unfortunate if you were to... leave too soon.”

His gaze lingered for a fraction of a second, the corner of his lips twitching—half smile, half warning.

“Yes... yes,” she murmured in astonishment.

How did he know I almost fell asleep?

Are there cameras everywhere?

The thought sent a chill through her.

I must be careful from now on.

He nodded and left as silently as he had come.

She returned to the room, dried off, dressed, and sat at the table. The smell of food instantly awakened her hunger—her stomach cramped, her mouth filled with saliva.

She began a prayer, then hesitated.

Can I trust even the food here? Why was I brought here? What is this care for? What if something has been added to it?

She inhaled deeply.

All right. I'll pretend to eat. Let them think I trust them.

But how, if she was being watched?

Refusing might draw suspicion.

What do I do? I'm so hungry...

She still had rusks and a few cans in her backpack—the ones she'd taken from the shop. She discreetly dropped the food from the tray under the table, placed the rusks on her plate, and began chewing them with exaggerated pleasure, as though dining in a Michelin-starred restaurant.

Michelin restaurant...

She smiled faintly.

Once, she had been a very wealthy woman. Together with her husband—a financial magnate—they had flown abroad on their private jet to sample rare dishes in the world's finest restaurants.

That life was long gone.

The world had changed beyond recognition: first the virus, then war, and now this explosion. People had stopped resisting. Technology had burned the spirit out of them. Children were raised on smartphones, damaging their development. Aggression was cultivated, and teenagers killed one another for amusement.

Her thoughts carried her far from the present.

Her head dropped onto the table, and sleep took her quietly.

She never reached the soft bed. She never finished her prayer.

She simply fell asleep.

In her dream, her son appeared.

His laughter sounded like music to her wounded heart. She reached for him, but he slipped away, vanishing into an abyss.

"Mom, help me!" he cried.

The desperate call pierced her soul.

Maryam screamed and woke up.

Tears streamed down her face. Everything that had been building inside her—exhaustion, pain, fear—burst forth. She sobbed until her strength gave out, then fell asleep again—this time without dreams, in a heavy, lifeless sleep.

She woke early.

Outside, hammers thudded, saws rang. People were working.

She went to the window. The same bleak scene. Nothing had changed.

This was no dream.

This was the new, harsh reality.

She washed up and studied her reflection. A stranger stared back—her features sharpened, marked by suffering. Nature had blessed her with youth; at forty, she had looked barely thirty. But now, quiet, stubborn pain had settled in her large eyes. Her lips were tightly pressed together. Silver strands glimmered in her dark hair—ones that hadn't been there yesterday.

She knelt and prayed fervently—for the living, for her son, for herself. The words poured out, sincere and desperate.

A knock sounded.

"Come in," she said, rising.

The door opened, and a man in a strict suit entered. His hair was neatly styled, and a mysterious smile was on his face.

She recognized him, the same man who had accompanied her upon arrival.

"Good morning. I'm glad to see you again," he said calmly.

"My name is Mikhail. Are you ready to talk?"

She nodded, hiding her anxiety.

"Yes... I'm ready. What do you want from me? Why am I here?"

Mikhail sat down, never taking his eyes off her. His dark, piercing gaze seemed to scan her, reading every crack in her armor.

"You're here because you are not like the others," he said, gesturing toward the dugouts outside. "Otherwise, you would be there."

He paused, studying her face.

"There is something very important within you—for us. Don't ask questions yet. Everything in its time."

Then he smiled.

"Have breakfast. And please—no more of last night's foolishness. If you keep that up, you'll drag every cockroach from the neighboring dugouts into your room."

His gaze shifted to the tray.

"Your breakfast."

Only now did Maryam notice it—fragrant pastries and coffee. Her stomach betrayed her with a growl.

"See? Even your body agrees with me," he smiled. "Don't resist. Eat. I'll be watching."

It was unpleasant to eat under his gaze, but she had no choice. Hunger twisted her insides. She sat, murmured a short prayer, and began to eat.

"Mariam," he said gently, "eat without fear. We're in a hurry."

"In a hurry for what?" she asked, biting into a warm bun and sipping aromatic coffee with milk.

Milk? Where did they get milk?

Powdered, perhaps... surely no cows survived.

Still, the coffee was exquisite.

Strength returned to her. Warmth filled her chest, and for a fleeting moment, it felt as though this was all just a bad dream.

Mikhail noticed the change and smiled slightly.

"You see," he said softly. "It's not as frightening as it seems."

"Now change your clothes, and I'll take you to our senior."

Change? Easy to say...

Her own clothes lay in the corner, worn and sour-smelling after weeks without washing. Putting them back on felt impossible.

He followed her gaze.

"Don't worry. You'll find everything you need in the wardrobe."

She raised an eyebrow, opened it—and froze.

Inside was a treasure: a flawless sports outfit, skirts, T-shirts, sweaters, jeans, and an elegant dress. Shoes—sneakers, heels, cozy boots in a drawer—underwear.

Everything fit perfectly.

How did they get all this?

Perhaps their leader has the answers.

Mikhail watched her silently.

"Are you going to keep staring at me?" she asked, mildly annoyed.

He blinked.

"I need to change."

"Oh—yes. Of course," he said, embarrassed. "Use the bathroom. I'll wait here."

She chose jeans and a sweater and stepped out.

Mikhail looked at her appraisingly. She had always been athletic; even at forty, her figure remained slender. Hunger and stress had made her leaner still, but the jeans fit perfectly.

How did they guess my size?

“Are you going to keep staring?” she asked, blushing. “Shall we go?”

He looked at her seriously.

“I’m not looking at your body,” Mikhail said calmly. “I see your Light—burning brighter than ever.”

“Light...?”

“Yes. Light.”

“Did you not know that every human emits Light?” he continued. “Man is God’s creation, and God is Light. So, man, made in His image, is also Light. Why are you surprised? Don’t your books speak of this? You pray so much, yet don’t know such simple things.”

He smiled faintly.

“That’s enough for today. Our senior will explain the rest.”

Her heart pounded. She felt as though she was being drawn into a game she didn’t understand.

“And if I refuse?”

He smiled, a flash of seriousness crossing his eyes.

“Then you will never know what your choice could have changed. And don’t forget your son. The knowledge we offer may be very useful to you.”

An undeniable argument, she thought, and followed Mikhail out.

CHAPTER 5
ARIZAL
THE PATH TO KNOWLEDGE

Mikhail stopped before a massive oak door.

Where did they get materials like this? The thought flickered through her mind.

Don't get distracted, she scolded herself, forcing her attention back to the present.

"Come in," a voice said.

Mikhail opened the door and, with a courteous gesture, let Maryam enter first.

"Thank you, Mikhail," the man said.

Mikhail nodded and stepped out, carefully closing the door behind him.

Maryam froze on the threshold.

Something inexplicable held her in place. It was not fear, but a reverent tremor that made her heart falter and her legs grow heavy. She couldn't bring herself to lift her gaze, as though the floor itself were drawing her downward, anchoring her in that moment.

The air in the room felt charged—not physically, but perceptually—as if every molecule vibrated with concealed energy. A strange numbness settled over her body; even the smallest movement seemed almost impossible. And yet, at the same time, warm currents began to move through her veins.

She silently called out to God. The paralysis eased slightly—just enough to allow her, at last, to raise her eyes.

“Hello,” she said, meeting his gaze.

“Hello, Maryam. Please, come in and take a seat,” he replied, watching her closely.

Maryam lowered herself into a chair near the desk, unease tightening her chest. There was something about this man that made her entire being draw inward, bracing itself.

Gathering her courage, she looked at him again.

He sat opposite a computer. Beside him lay a large black book—one he had clearly been reading when they entered.

“Maryam, don’t worry. Your son is safe. And it is quite possible you will see him very soon.”

The words sent her springing to her feet.

“Really?” she cried. “I’ll be able to see my son? How? When?”

“First of all, that depends on you,” he said calmly. “You must learn composure and restraint.”

A warm smile touched his lips, unexpectedly softening his otherwise severe features.

Maryam found herself studying him: wavy hair streaked with silver at the temples; dark eyes with a faint metallic glint; a classically shaped nose; full lips; and a distinctive cleft in his chin that gave his face a striking expressiveness. Of average height, with flawless posture and an athletic build, he left a powerful, lasting impression.

It was as though he had read her thoughts.

"Allow me to introduce myself," he said. "My name is Arizal."

What an unusual name, she thought.

"Maryam, we have been observing you since you were a child."

"What?" she exclaimed. "How is that possible? Where? How were you watching me?"

"Maryam," he said gently, "I have already told you—you must learn restraint. Patience. Pause."

He glanced at her posture.

"And pay attention to how you're sitting."

"How am I sitting?" she asked, surprised. "I sat where you pointed."

"Yes, that's correct. But your posture—your legs are crossed. That obstructs the circulation of energy."

He stepped closer, sat beside her, and took her hands.

"Close your eyes. Uncross your arms and legs. Relax..."

Relax?! Maryam scoffed inwardly.

That's rich. He tells me to relax when my husband's whereabouts are unknown, the world is collapsing, my son has been taken, and I'm supposed to relax? He must be out of his mind.

"I'm not out of my mind," he said suddenly.

She flinched.

“How did you know what I was thinking?”

“You wear your thoughts on your face,” he replied with a smile.

“Maryam, do you want to learn? To find your son and bring him back? If so, stop resisting. You must relax and trust God.”

I’ll never stop resisting, she thought, but I’ll try to relax.

She closed her eyes, setting a firm rule for herself: the main thing is to stay in control.

Arizal took her hands and inhaled deeply.

In that instant, warm, exquisitely pleasant currents rushed through her body, from the crown of her head down to her heels and back again. The sensation was extraordinary, as if every cell were filling with light while anxiety dissolved inside the flow.

She wanted this state to last as long as possible.

Another moment and I think I’ll lose consciousness, she thought, drifting in a sea of bliss.

“That’s enough,” he said softly. “For today, this is sufficient. We’ll leave things as they are for now. I will help you. And for now... we will nourish ourselves together,” Arizal added cryptically.

“Nourish ourselves with what?” she asked, pulled abruptly back to reality.

He said nothing.

With effort, she pulled herself out of the state. Strangely enough, she wanted him to touch her again.

Nonsense, she scolded herself. My son is missing, and I’m indulging in questionable sensations.

Trying to shake it off, she changed the subject.

“What book is that on your desk? Before the catastrophe, I loved reading.”

“That book is not for you yet,” he replied. “The day will come when you’ll be able to read it.”

Arizal pressed a button, and Mikhail entered the room.

“Mikhail, please escort Maryam to her room.”

Maryam was relieved to leave the office. The space felt oppressive—as if it compressed reality around her, leaving only that strange, almost hypnotic voice and the sensation of all-pervading energy.

In her room, she sank into a chair, lost in thought.

What was that? She had never experienced anything like it.

She felt inexplicably drawn to him—but not as a woman to a man. Never. She would not betray her husband even in thought, not for a second. This was something else, beyond rational understanding: a desire to merge with him on some subtle, energetic level—to become a single radiant sphere of light.

In his office, he had filled her to the brim with those currents, and she remained in a state of light euphoria—a pure, almost childlike joy she had long forgotten. She wanted to sing and dance.

To her shame, the pain for her son was no longer tearing her heart apart as it had before. In its place came certainty—a quiet certainty that everything would be all right.

But now, alone again, the euphoria slowly dissipated, giving way to anxiety and fear. She began to shiver; an inner cold shook her body.

Maryam went to the bathroom, filled the tub with hot water, and sank into the soothing warmth, trying to calm the tremors. Gradually, her body relaxed; it became easier to breathe.

Wrapped in a thick terry robe, she crawled under the blanket. Warmth enveloped her gently, and she fell into a deep, dreamless sleep.

In the morning, a knock sounded at the door.

Maryam opened her eyes, trying to remember where she was. Reality returned quickly.

"Come in," she said, her voice hoarse with sleep.

The door opened, and Mikhail appeared.

"Good morning, Maryam," he said warmly.

"Good morning," she replied, stretching and shaking off the remnants of sleep.

"How did you sleep?"

"Thank you—well."

"I brought you breakfast," he said, placing an elegant tray on the table.

Maryam glanced at the food and gave a small shake of her head.

"Thank you, Mikhail, but I don't really have an appetite today."

"That's normal," he replied calmly. "Your body is filled with energy, so you don't feel hunger. A cleansing process is underway. The body experiences a kind of withdrawal."

"What kind of withdrawal?" she asked, surprised.

Mikhail sat in the chair opposite her.

"You see, Maryam, the human body is a divine structure—a vessel for the soul. When purification begins, the body experiences discomfort. The vessel expands, growing capable of receiving a greater measure of Divine Light, and that process is not always pleasant. Don't worry—this state is temporary. You will manage."

He slid the tray closer. In a delicate dish lay dates; beside them stood cups of tea and coffee.

"Thank you very much, Mikhail," she said gratefully. "Tell me, please—what are the plans for today? When will I learn something about my son?"

"After breakfast, you will begin your lessons with Arizal," he replied, then left the room.

Maryam went to the bathroom, washed her face, brushed her teeth, changed into a tracksuit, and then knelt to pray:

"Lord, give me the strength not to be led into temptation.

Grant me spiritual sight, so I may recognize falsehood.

Do not let me stray from the path.

Lord, protect my soul from evil.

Save my husband, wherever he may be, and protect our son. Do not let him perish."

After the prayer, her soul felt lighter—as if a heavy burden had lifted just enough to let her breathe.

She still wasn't hungry, but Mikhail's words sounded convincing.

All right. I'll do it.

Reluctantly, she ate a date and drank some tea.

Done, she thought, just as a soft knock sounded at the door.

Mikhail appeared again.

"Maryam, are you ready? They're waiting."

She stood and followed him.

This time, their path did not lead to Arizal's office, but two floors higher. There, a spacious, bright room awaited them—furnished with striking simplicity: only a bookcase, a table, and two chairs.

Mikhail left her alone.

Approaching the shelves, Maryam was surprised to see that the books were written in an unfamiliar language. Her fingers instinctively reached for one—but she immediately pulled her hand back, sensing a faint warmth radiating from the cover.

The same large black book lay on the table—the one Maryam had seen during her first visit to Arizal's office. Unable to resist, she picked it up.

Instantly, warmth flooded her body. Her head spun, and she swayed.

"What are you doing?" a stern voice rang out. "Did I not warn you that it is too early for you to touch this book? Your vessel is not yet ready to receive its wisdom. It can be dangerous."

"And what would happen if I opened it?" she asked quietly.

"There are several possibilities," he replied.

"First, you would temporarily lose the ability to study, and deep sorrow would overtake you.

Second—imagine placing your fingers into a live electrical socket."

"What would you feel?" he asked.

"Nothing pleasant," she said, with a faint, involuntary smile.

"Exactly. That is why we will not rush. For now, you should not touch this book."

He paused, then added calmly:

"Now, let us not waste time and begin our studies. First, you must master the language in which these books are written."

"Arizal," Maryam asked, "what language is this?"

"What matters is not its name," he replied, "but the knowledge and power contained within these texts. Our alphabet is unique. By studying it, you connect to a source of energy. By reading, you are filled with it."

"And how will this help save my son?"

"It will affect not only your son's fate," he answered enigmatically, "but the fate of the entire world."

"How is that possible?"

"You will learn gradually," he replied, "as you study with us the structure of existence."

"But can the world truly be changed by studying the structure of creation through books?" she objected. "Is it not God who grants us knowledge—as a reward for good deeds and righteous actions?"

"No matter how hard you try," Arizal said, "you cannot always remain good. Even saints are not good at all times; they, too, are subject to temptation. As long as you inhabit a physical body, you will be exposed to it in one form or another. But the ability to struggle always exists. While a person lives, they can resist. And afterwards, each receives what they have earned."

"But the saints say, 'Where there is complexity, there is not a single angel; where there is simplicity, there are hundreds," Maryam countered.

"That is true," Arizal smiled. "But to reach such a level, one must become a saint. And you are still far from that. So, we will not leap three steps at once. We will ascend slowly—step by step."

"Very well," Maryam nodded. "I am ready. With God's help, I hope I will succeed. Since childhood, I have never had a talent for languages."

"The more difficult something is," Arizal replied evenly, "the Lighter we earn through it."

By the end of the first hour, Maryam's head was throbbing.

"That will be enough for today," the teacher said, noticing her fatigue. "But this knowledge is extraordinarily important. The energetic fields of these letters possess intelligence—the same intelligence that exists within us. Everything in existence, from stones and stars to plants, animals, and human beings—every particle—is not only made of energy but is also a vessel of inexhaustible intelligent force."

"When we use these powerful energetic sources to fulfill the principle 'Love your neighbor as yourself,' conditions are created for harmony and health in the lives of those who believe in it."

"Do you now understand how vital knowledge is for saving your son?"

Maryam remained silent. Her thoughts spun.

God... she thought. Only He can help me. But then why am I here? Why have these people, this strange knowledge, this pressure, become part of my path?

"Only God can help me," she finally said aloud, her voice quieter than she expected. "Not your knowledge, but prayer and fasting. That is the path to saving my son. And I believe He will help me."

Arizal did not answer at once. He leaned back in his chair and looked at her with that particular expression in which patience and gentle sadness were intertwined, as though he perceived not only her words, but every unspoken fear tormenting her soul.

"Yes," he agreed at last. "God will help. But how? He cannot simply transport you to your son, or your son to you. The age of open miracles ended centuries ago. Now God acts through intermediaries. He sends instruments, people, or sometimes objects. So why is it so difficult for you to accept that perhaps God sent us to help you?"

"Do you not know: 'Nothing moves below unless it is decreed above?"

"Yes... Perhaps," she conceded.

"Listen, Maryam," Arizal continued. "In ancient times, this knowledge was hidden from humanity, sealed until the end of days. Now the time has come to reveal it. But not everyone is ready to receive it. Only those who seek purification and wish to ascend."

"Why did you choose to reveal it to me?" she asked. "What have I done to deserve such an honor?"

“You have always sought communion with God,” he replied. “And we have seen it.”

“You saw?” she exclaimed. “How could you see it, if I didn’t even know you existed?”

“It is not yet time for you to know that,” he replied. “You rush too much. And haste in this work brings consequences. It can throw you back like a splinter struck by an axe—several levels down—and we would have to lift you again. So let us not hurry.”

“All right,” she sighed. “Forgive me, thoughts of my son give me no peace. I keep rushing events. If only I could see him... touch him... speak with him, it would be so much easier.”

Arizal frowned.

“You keep speaking about yourself: I, I, I.”

“How can I speak of myself,” she cried, “when I am talking about my son? How can you not understand? I am a mother! While I am here, warm, fed, safe, my son... what of him? Is he eating? Is he alive? Is he being mistreated? How can you not see that this is tearing me apart?”

Maryam broke down in tears.

Arizal waited until she calmed, then approached and gently stroked her head. A warm wave of protection and care enveloped her, and gradually, peace filled her soul.

“Maryam,” he said softly, “your emotions and self-pity will not help your son. The deeper you sink into grief, the more darkness fills your heart, and then nothing luminous can reach him. Suffering is heavy, but it purifies the soul. Most people turn to God in suffering, not in joy. You are different from many, but you are not without sin.

You must not suffer, you must act. Work on yourself. Cleanse your earthly vessel."

"What must I do?" she asked, pain trembling in her voice.

"Pray. Study with me. And try to obey me."

That will be difficult, she thought. How can I obey a man I barely know, who claims he can help save my son? And how can I know he is not my enemy? Oh God... help me understand all of this.

Arizal looked at her intently, not merely seeing her, but penetrating the depth of her being.

"Maryam, doubt is good," he said. "But it slows the path to knowledge."

She met his gaze.

How unusual his eyes were... Yesterday they had seemed almost black—today they were deep blue, like the evening sky.

"Do you wear contact lenses?" she asked impulsively.

He laughed, lightly, sincerely, dissolving the tension.

"Maryam, you are charmingly spontaneous. I speak to you of things that alter one's perception of the world, and you think about my eyes."

"I'm not thinking about your eyes!" she protested, blushing. "They were black yesterday—and today they're blue, like the evening sky."

"You imagined it," he said gently. "Yesterday we were in my office—it was dark. Here, on the second floor, there is much more light. You simply saw them from a different angle. Enough about me—let us continue. Although I believe today's lesson is sufficient."

"No, no!" Maryam objected quickly. "I still have strength, and I'm eager to learn—please, continue!"

He smiled—almost fatherly, yet in that smile lay both wisdom and a faint amusement at her impatience.

"No, Maryam. Your vessel is not yet ready to receive more. One cannot pour more into it than it can hold. Do you understand?"

"And what happens if I do receive more?" she persisted.

"The vessel shatters," he answered calmly.

"And what does that mean?"

"I will explain it at our next lesson. For now, you must rest."

Arizal pressed a button on the desk. Soon, Mikhail appeared.

"Mikhail, we are finished for today. Please escort Maryam to her room."

As soon as they left the study, her head began to throb. It felt as though she had been filled with something invisible, and carrying that weight was not easy. Perhaps this was exactly what Arizal meant when he said the vessel could hold only as much as it was able.

Mikhail walked quietly beside her, his gaze resting on her face with barely perceptible compassion.

"Do not worry," he said gently. "Soon your vessel will expand, and you will be able to hold more knowledge."

She looked at him in surprise.

"How do you always know what I'm thinking?" she asked. "Can you read my thoughts?"

"No, Maryam," he smiled. "We cannot read your thoughts. That is permitted only to angels."

A remarkable warmth radiated from him, stirring an inexplicable trust. Mikhail escorted her to her room.

"You should rest," he advised. "Later, you may take a short walk."

"I can go for a walk?" she asked in surprise.

"Of course. Why not? You are not a prisoner here."

"I thought you wouldn't allow it."

"Maryam," Mikhail said softly, "believe me, no one is holding you here by force. Knowledge does not tolerate coercion. If you do not wish to receive it, we cannot give it to you."

"Oh... free will," she remembered.

"Yes," he nodded. "God granted humanity the right to choose."

"But between what and what must I choose?" she asked, looking intently into his eyes. "Between good and evil? Who are you, really?"

"We are people who sincerely wish to help you," Mikhail replied calmly.

"I hope not in wolves' clothing," she murmured.

"All right, Maryam. Rest."

When the door closed behind him, Maryam sat down on the edge of the bed—and, without realizing it, drifted into sleep.

In her dream, she was walking with two men. Their laughter and lighthearted banter filled the air. Suddenly, one of them lifted her into his arms and said, "You need to be cleansed."

He carried her to a lake and immersed her three times in the cold water. Trembling, she pressed herself against him. When he set her down, Maryam lifted her eyes to the sky—and saw a Face gazing at her. Gradually, the image dissolved, leaving only enormous eyes staring directly into her soul. Beside them appeared inscriptions in an unfamiliar language. She tried to read them—and woke up.

I must learn this ancient language as soon as possible, to understand what is being asked of me, Maryam decided firmly.

Her stomach growled, reminding her that since morning, she had eaten nothing but a single date.

A soft knock at the door pulled her from her thoughts.

Mikhail entered, carrying a tray fragrant with inviting aromas. Steam rose from a bowl of rich broth; beside it lay crusty bread and a cup of black tea.

After thanking him and saying a brief prayer, she ate with genuine pleasure. He waited patiently until she finished.

"Thank you," she said. "May we go for a walk?"

"Yes, of course," he replied. "I'll accompany you." Maryam stood, whispered a prayer of gratitude, and stepped outside into the courtyard with Mikhail.

CHAPTER 6
AN UNEXPECTED MEETING

A cold December wind cut straight through to the bone. The sky was sealed beneath a blanket of gray clouds, no snow, no sun, only dampness and emptiness. A thin layer of frost coated the ground, crunching softly beneath her feet.

Maryam wondered how much time had passed since the explosion. A month? Six weeks? Everything had merged into one endless chain of days, in which thoughts of her son gave her no peace—not for a single moment.

Where is he now...?

She drew a deep breath and noticed that Mikhail had tactfully fallen behind, understanding that she needed to be alone.

Maryam walked slowly along the worn path when suddenly someone grabbed her legs, and she heard a cheerful child's voice:

"Aunt Maryam!"

She startled and turned around.

Yulia stood before her—tousled, her nose red from the frost.

"Oh my God! Yulia! I'm so happy to see you!" Maryam cried, pulling the girl close.

"And where is your mother?"

"She's over there with Alexandra. They're helping set up the dugouts."

"Could you take me to them, please?" Maryam asked.

Yulia happily took her hand, and they set off along the winding path.

Maryam's heart tightened painfully as she looked around. Dark patches on the ground told the story of a place that had once been alive and bustling, now slowly being reclaimed by nature. People moved through the small settlement like ants, working tirelessly.

Cleanup was in full swing. Men and women cleared debris, leveled the ground, and prepared sites for new temporary shelters. Everything looked strikingly coordinated—each person seemed to understand that this hard labor was necessary to rebuild their lives and their future.

How did they manage to unite and organize everyone so quickly? Maryam wondered.

At last, they reached a group of women.

"Mom!" Yulia shouted. "Look who I brought!"

One of the women lifted her head, wiping her face with a scarf.

"Who, Yulia?" she asked.

"Look!" Yulia bounced with excitement.

The woman stepped forward—and froze.

"Maryam... I can't believe my eyes. It's you! God, how glad I am!" She rushed toward her. "You're alive!"

The women embraced and stepped aside. Anna studied her friend carefully.

"Did you find your son?"

"No," Maryam replied.

Anna hugged her more tightly.

"I found out something. He's not here. They're on the other side of the city."

"But there's radiation there!" Maryam cried in horror.

"No," Anna said quietly. "In that area, the radiation is minimal. They're fed. They live in good conditions. They're being trained."

Maryam felt a surge of relief—but one look at Anna's face made her stop short.

"There's a 'but,' isn't there?"

"Yes," Anna said. "They're doing everything they can to make the children forget God."

"What do you mean?" Maryam asked.

"They give them ideal conditions and convince them that man rules everything, and that there is no God. Humanity holds power over life and death. Society is divided into castes: worker bees, an elite, and a single leader over the entire hive. And if the children want to join the elite instead of remaining bees, they must abandon this 'heresy' about God and live for the glory of their Leader."

"My merciful God..." Maryam whispered, covering her face. "Has the end of times truly come? Is what was written in all the Holy Scriptures happening before our eyes?"

Tears streamed down her cheeks.

"Lord, do not let my son stray from the path. Preserve his soul."

“It won’t be easy to get there,” Anna warned softly. “You’ll have to pass through parts of the city with the infected—mutants. If you’re contaminated, you won’t be able to help him at all.”

“What am I supposed to do?” Maryam cried in despair.

“You’ll need a special protective suit,” Anna said gravely. “But even that offers no guarantee. These people are extremely dangerous. If they catch you, no suit will save you.”

“But I have to try.”

“Yes. But don’t rush. You need to think everything through carefully. For now, help us here. There’s still so much to do—build shelters, sew clothes, pillows, blankets from whatever fabric survived. It’s getting colder every day. We have to prepare for winter.”

She smiled faintly.

“The stoves in the dugouts are already built and working well. We just need to add a bit of comfort.”

“How can I help?” Maryam asked without hesitation. “I’m ready to do anything.”

Anna glanced around.

“Look at how many children there are. They have nothing to do—they wander aimlessly. The older ones help with cleanup, but the younger ones... we’re constantly distracted, trying to keep them from getting hurt. Could you organize something like a daycare for them?”

“With pleasure!” Maryam brightened. “Just tell me where to start.”

"Wonderful. First, wash the children and take them to the afternoon lunch. Then keep them occupied."

Together with Yulia, Maryam gathered about fifteen children, aged three to eleven. The older ones were already helping the adults.

Water was scarce—barely enough for drinking, let alone washing.

But they found water for my bath, she thought.

A familiar young man approached.

"I was told to let you know—there's water for washing in a barrel behind that building," he said, pointing toward the canteen.

"Wait—what's your name?" Maryam asked.

"Hakim," he replied, and ran off.

She and Yulia followed the direction and found a large barrel fixed to the wall at chest height, fitted with a tap. Beneath it burned a small brazier with glowing coals to keep the water from freezing.

"Who took care of all this?" Maryam wondered aloud.

"Hakim!" Yulia chirped. "I saw him lighting the fire under the barrel."

Once again, Maryam marveled at the thoughtfulness surrounding her. Even in a place where every day was a struggle for survival, someone found time and strength for small miracles—for warm water, neatly stacked firewood, and places for children to play.

After washing all the children to a cheerful little song—"Wash, wash, scrub it clean..."—Maryam led them to lunch. The meal was simple: bread, potatoes with canned meat, and tea with condensed milk. The children were content and tired.

She called Hakim and asked, "Is there a free dugout where we could organize a daycare?"

He thought for a moment, then nodded and led them to a spacious dugout with a one-story extension above it.

We could make a classroom here, Maryam thought as she looked around. And downstairs—a bedroom.

For now, together with the children, they dragged in old mattresses that had miraculously survived the explosion. Settling onto them, the children grew quiet in anticipation.

Maryam stood by the window, from which a view of the recovering town opened up.

"Today," she said softly, "I will tell you a fairy tale—about a Little Bird."

Her voice, warm and gentle, filled the room.

The Tale of the Little Bird

Long, long ago, high in the mountains, there lived a little bird—a charming creature with a dainty head, a colorful crest, and a sharp little beak.

More than anything else in the world, the little bird loved to fly and to play at dawn with the rays of the rising sun. Soaring up to the mountain peaks, she would plunge like a stone alongside a majestic waterfall, and below, after bathing in the quiet, crystal-clear water, she loved to gaze at her reflection in the mirror-like surface.

One day, having flown to the very top of a mountain, the little bird noticed an old village far below. Curiosity stirred within her—she wanted to fly down and see how people lived.

An old raven had always warned her never to go near humans.

But the Little Bird's curiosity prevailed, and she flew down to the village.

Below, the air proved completely different—warm and still, unlike the thin, cold air of her mountain home, where fierce winds often raged. There it was warm and quiet, fragrant with flowers. It was spring. The village lay in the foothills; the flowers had already bloomed, and spring had fully come into its own.

The little bird delighted in the warmth and the silence.

Suddenly, she saw a man.

She had never encountered humans before—she only knew from the raven that one must never approach them. The little bird was frightened and froze. Afraid to move, she stared at him in terror.

The man appeared to be a wealthy merchant, traveling to the city to sell his goods. When he saw the Little Bird, he was struck by her beauty—never before had he seen such a bird.

She had a beautiful, multicolored crest that shimmered in the sunlight with every color of the rainbow, and a small, sharp beak. The man gazed at the Little Bird in admiration, and a powerful desire arose within him for her to belong to him.

Throwing a cloth over her, he seized her and placed her in a cage.

The little bird, who had never known what a cage was, was horrified. She beat her wings against the metal bars and begged to be set free, to return to her beloved mountain.

But when the man heard her beautiful voice, he desired this treasure even more.

He brought her to his home and placed the cage in the most beautiful spot. He poured grain for her, filled her bowl with water, and ordered a goldsmith to craft a golden cage adorned with precious stones. He decorated her crest with fine pearls.

Each evening, he played music for her on various instruments and asked her to sing, to entertain his guests.

But the little bird longed deeply for her homeland.

Every day, she reproached herself for not listening to the old raven and for flying down to the people. Now she saw the true nature of humans—they were cruel and selfish. They did only what pleased them: they ate and drank, slept, dressed in fine clothes, and, having everything, shared nothing with those who had nothing—no food, no drink, no clothing.

She saw how people deceived one another.

Once, she watched her owner greet his guests with exaggerated courtesy, showering them with gifts—but when they left, he spoke of them with bitterness and contempt.

Not once did she see humans offer praise to the Creator.

High in the mountains, every living creature glorified the Creator. All, in their own way and in every manner, sang a song of praise:

Glory, glory to the Creator,

Who created the universe!

Glory, glory to the Creator,

Who breathed life into us!

And we thank You for this!

And humans?

They rise in the morning, eat abundantly, go about their affairs, and never once remember the Creator.

Then the little bird realized that since she had fallen into human hands, she herself had not once remembered to sing the Song of Praise.

And she began to sing.

She sang so fervently to the Creator—of her sorrow, of her misfortune, of the people who no longer remembered Him—that the force of her prayer split the cage in two.

The little bird flew free.

As she flew, she looked like a small glowing sphere, for her heart burned with love for the Creator. The crest upon her tiny head shone like a radiant halo, and all who met her along the way marveled at the little bird with the great, blazing heart—so full of love for the Creator that even the metal bars of the cage could not withstand the power of her love for God.

When Maryam finished, silence filled the dugout. Only the soft breathing of the sleeping children remained.

"That's good," she whispered, gently tucking a blanket around the youngest girl. The child smiled faintly in her sleep, and Maryam's heart trembled with tenderness.

She sat there for a while, watching their peaceful faces.

"Thank You, Lord," she whispered.

Soon, the children began to stir.

"Come now, my dears," she said softly. "It's time to wake up. Let's go see Aunt Anna and Alexandra."

Outside, the evening cold had already settled in. Dusk fell quickly. Judging by the sun sinking toward the horizon, it was about five o'clock. Since the explosion, daylight seemed shorter, as if time itself had changed.

People finished their work and dispersed to their homes. Children looked around eagerly, searching for familiar faces.

Maryam spotted Anna and Alexandra by a fire.

"How was your day?" she asked.

"Tiring," Anna smiled, "but productive. A few more dugouts, and families can move in."

"And you?" Alexandra asked.

"We had a wonderful time with the children," Maryam replied. "They're so full of life... I almost forgot everything."

The women thanked her warmly.

"If it weren't for you, we'd have had to chase after the children all day."

Hakim appeared soon after.

"It's time," he reminded her.

Maryam nodded, kissed the children on the tops of their heads, and left them with their mothers.

"I'll come again tomorrow," she promised.

CHAPTER 7
THE VESSEL EXPANDS

In the room, Maryam quickly showered, washing away the dust of the day and the remnants of tension. She changed into clean clothes and sat in the armchair by the window. Outside, twilight was slowly deepening, painting the sky in rich shades of purple. Maryam sat, hugging her knees, waiting for someone to come for her. *"So much has happened this past month... It feels like a whole lifetime compressed into a single moment. How is my family? Where are they? What has happened to my husband?"* How I miss him now, his strong back, behind which I could always hide, his support. *Where is my son? Although Arizal assured me that physically he is fine, he is not hungry and has somewhere to sleep. That is comforting, yet how painful... I hope they haven't burned out his faith.* Maryam closed her eyes, took a deep breath, and whispered:

"I beseech You, Heavenly Father, Do not let us forget Your covenants.

Forgive the people their sins, For they know not what they do.

Heal the Earth from the evil of this world,

And save our children."

She prayed so fervently that she didn't notice Mikhail entering the room and quietly standing by the door.

"Excuse me," he said. "I knocked, but you were so absorbed that I didn't want to disturb you."

"It's nothing," Maryam replied, rising from her knees. "Are we going to Arizal?"

"No, first you need to eat something."

Mikhail placed a tray in front of her. Only then did she realize how hungry she was; she had spent the whole day with the children, completely forgetting herself. Now, her stomach demanded attention.

Maryam looked at him gratefully.

"Thank you, Mikhail, I won't keep you."

Dinner consisted of leaves of salad with olive oil and lemon, boiled potatoes, and most precious of all, coffee!

"Simple food allows the brain to work better," she watched with a smile as she devoured the food with obvious enjoyment. Maryam smiled back. For the first time in a long while, she truly tasted her food. The plate emptied quickly. She murmured a brief prayer of thanks, stood, and nodded to Mikhail.

"I'm ready."

They stepped into the corridor. It was half-lit; only a few lamps cast warm circles of light against the stone walls.

Arizal sat at his desk, absorbed in a book. Lamplight fell across the pages, lifting thin lines of ancient text out of the shadows. Maryam entered quietly and paused at the threshold, unwilling to disturb the hush. His eyes were fixed on the page, yet it felt as though his spirit hovered somewhere far beyond this world.

He finished reading, closed the book slowly, and lifted his gaze.

At once her whole body tightened, as if seized by an invisible force, while warm waves passed through her. The strange sensations made her head spin.

He smiled.

"Maryam. Come in. Sit down."

What a remarkable voice, she thought, watching him. He must sing beautifully.

"Yes," Arizal said, amusement flickering in his eyes. "I'll admit, I do sing rather well."

Oh... so he really can read minds? Maryam thought, startled.

She couldn't hold it back.

"How did you know what I was thinking?"

"When you drift into thought," he explained gently, "your face reflects everything. But enough about me. I know you've had a full day. You did well."

"It's true," Maryam said, brightening. "It was productive. But there's still so much to do, beds for the children in the daycare, and we need to set up a proper classroom..."

"Everything in its time," Arizal said thoughtfully.

"What you started there is good," he added. "Children must receive spiritual nourishment, the sprouts will not bear good fruit."

He leaned forward slightly.

"Now. Let's continue with the alphabet and try reading."

"With pleasure," Maryam replied, her eyes shining with anticipation.

An hour later, she knew every letter and could read short words—something that filled her with almost childish joy.

"The power of this alphabet is extraordinary," Arizal said. "By mastering it, you will learn to govern your emotions—and much more."

"But how can that be, if it's only letters?" she asked, bewildered.

"Yes, Maryam—you can. Believe me."

His voice softened.

"Now listen to me carefully."

He paused, his gaze drifting somewhere beyond the walls of the room, and then continued:

"The time has come for humanity to turn not toward the outer world, but toward the inner cosmos—the cosmos of thought. It is there, on the field of human thoughts, emotions, and relationships, that the great battle between light and darkness unfolds."

He fell silent for a moment.

"We are living through a time of global cleansing. That is why these horrors have occurred. Humanity has sunk into sin and refuses to learn from the examples of those who came before. Remember Sodom and Gomorrah—they reached the limit of corruption. Their egoism left no room for giving—only desire and pleasure. The consequences were inevitable. They were made from dust, and to dust they returned."

Maryam nodded slowly.

"Yes... I agree. And modern humanity—hasn't it come dangerously close to the same edge?"

"Exactly," Arizal said. "But we still have a chance to change everything. The knowledge you are receiving is not merely letters and words. It is a path toward understanding the true nature of reality—and a power capable of transforming the world."

He looked at her steadily.

"People must realize that the time has come to unite—to become one with the Creator. We are His lesser likeness, created in His image. If we truly comprehend this, perhaps the vessel can be corrected."

Maryam listened, sensing the depth of his words. She absorbed them like a sponge, afraid to miss even the slightest thread. And her soul demanded more.

She longed for knowledge the way a traveler in the desert longs for water—drinking in every word, filling herself to the brim. A vast thirst opened within her, not physical but spiritual: a hunger to understand.

She swallowed, her throat tight with emotion.

"Arizal," Maryam said hoarsely, "you promised you would tell me about the Breaking of the Vessel."

"I remember," he replied. "And now we have come to it."

He spoke with calm, measured clarity.

"Human beings are born with selfish desire. Their task on Earth is correction. They must free themselves from egoistic inclinations and learn to care and think not only of themselves, but of others."

He glanced toward the window and continued:

"The theory of the Big Bang has its explanation—but what I am speaking of did not occur here. It took place in the higher worlds. There truly was an explosion—only it was a spiritual one."

His voice softened, yet each word carried weight.

"The Creator had to restrict Himself, for the world could not withstand the abundance of Light He bestowed. The spiritual vessels were unable to endure the pressure of that Divine Light. They shattered and fell from higher realms into lower worlds, continuing to fragment as they descended."

He met her gaze.

"Maryam—everything I am telling you happened before the creation of our world."

Then, slowly, he revealed the law underlying it all:

"You must understand this: within the Creator there is no desire to receive—only the desire to give. He created us as vessels to receive His gifts. He gives; we receive. But if we take without giving in return, shame is born. To prevent this, the desire to receive must be transformed into the desire to give."

He offered a simple example.

"Imagine you visit someone after you have already eaten, and your hosts have prepared a meal. You do not want food and politely refuse. But the host insists, and, wishing to bring him joy, you sit and eat. In that moment, something important occurs: you receive the food, yes—but at the same time you give pleasure to the host by accepting his offering."

Maryam frowned slightly, concentrating.

"It's an interesting comparison... but I'm not entirely sure where it leads."

"It reveals the path of spiritual development," Arizal said quietly,

"from egoism to altruism, from receiving to giving, from darkness to light.

His tone grew more intense, though never loud.

"Humanity must become one whole and hold a single intention: to correct the world through good deeds. People must, as it were, be bound together, and the bond will be intention: a shared striving toward one purpose, toward the Creator."

He continued, unwavering:

"A person may try to walk the path of commandments, prayer, fasting, and good works, yet temptation remains. At some point, weakness appears. Sometimes it comes disguised as pride: the thought, I overcame myself. I conquered anger. I conquered laziness. I did well.

"And the very moment that thought flashes, 'I am good, I succeeded'—the dark side awakens. It never sleeps. It waits for the smallest crack. Let the door open even a fraction, and those forces will enter."

His eyes held hers.

"What matters is recognizing this in time and opposing it through humility before God, by accepting your weakness and repenting. You must not delay. Prolonged shame before the Creator can lead to a deeper fall—into depression—and then you close yourself entirely to the Creator's Light."

He leaned closer.

“Do you hear me, Maryam? Acceptance, and humility.”

“Yes,” she said quietly. “I hear you, Arizal. But it is one thing to understand everything you are saying with the mind, and quite another to accept it with the heart. You cannot understand me. I am a mother.”

“I do understand you,” Arizal replied. “And in order to help your son, you must submit to the will of the Creator—to His decision.”

“I have submitted.”

“Not completely. You are suffering.”

"But how can I avoid it? What can I do with myself? I cannot tear my heart out and stop suffering."

"No one asks you to do that. You must become stronger. If you were sent now to save your son, you would not manage; the forces are too unequal. You cannot even imagine who you will be dealing with. That is why we are sent to help you cleanse, rise, and become stronger. Do you understand?"

"I don’t know," she answered wearily.

"Maryam, when you constantly

repeat: 'I am tired, I am suffering, I am a mother,' this is not humility, but egoism," Arizal said softly. "You think more about your suffering than about your son’s suffering. This is the essence of the 'Shattering of the Vessel.' In this state, you will not be able to expand your spiritual vessel and accept a greater amount of Divine Light. And if you tried to take in more knowledge now, as when you took my 'Black Book' from the table, you would not be able to contain a large amount of Light (knowledge) in your unprepared vessel. This would lead to its destruction and cause temporary spiritual chaos in your soul. But this is not bad; in time, you would have an even greater desire for knowledge, only it would take more time, and we have little time."

"I understand," she smiled.

"Remember," Arizal continued, "the Creator made us free to choose. That is why we need 'imperfect' vessels, which can both receive light and resist it."

He used a vivid metaphor:

"Imagine trying to fill a fragile glass with water under strong pressure. If the glass is not strong enough, it will break, and the water will spill. Exactly this happened with spiritual structures; their fragility led to chaos, but this created the opportunity for growth and correction."

"Do you understand now what the Shattering of the Vessel means?"

"I think so," Maryam replied slowly, as if tasting each word. "The Shattering of the Vessel is not a catastrophe, but a part of the Divine plan. Thanks to it, it became possible to create a world with the possibility of free choice.

Give humans the opportunity to participate in repairing the world through spiritual practice and good deeds."

"Yes, Maryam, you are doing well, you understand it correctly. We must all unite, and nothing must divide us. After all, each of us is a fragment of that vessel. And only together can we begin its restoration." Maryam nodded silently.

In her mind, a new picture of the world was gradually taking shape, not flat as before, but three-dimensional, threaded with invisible connections and meanings. She felt a strange new sensation stirring within her: not fear of the unknown, but a quiet, confident readiness to move forward.

CHAPTER 8
THE STRANGER

Returning to her room, Maryam literally collapsed into the chair. Her head throbbed with tension, and her body trembled with a slight shiver. Summoning her strength, she made her way to the bathroom. After washing her face with cold water, she lifted her gaze to the mirror. In the reflection, an unfamiliar woman: a weary face, shadows under her eyes, but... her eyes were alight. Not feverishly, not desperately, but steadily, as if a quiet, unextinguishable flame had been kindled within. Returning to the bedroom, she put on her robe, dropped to her knees, and whispered:

"Lord... Heavenly Father.

I do not know why You are giving me all of this. But I surrender to You—

Not as I want, but as You will..."

Finally, she reached the bed and slipped under the blanket. Warmth enveloped her, her breathing evened out, and without realizing it, Maryam drifted into a wondrous, almost living dream. It was so vivid that it felt less like a dream and more like reality.

There she found herself in a spacious room with Arizal, her teacher. And can you guess what he was teaching her there?

You wouldn't believe it—how to fly! Yes, exactly!

He was teaching her to levitate!!! Using those very mysterious letters from the magical alphabet and spoken words, he rose into the air to a height of about one and a half to two meters.

She could hardly believe her eyes. But when it was her turn, she managed it too. Uttering special words and visualizing the mysterious letters in her mind, she felt herself lift off the ground. Of course, her success was more modest—only about a meter high—but it was a true miracle. The air around her seemed pliant, obedient to her thoughts and words. It was an indescribable feeling of freedom.

The dream faded not abruptly, but gradually, leaving behind a delicate trace, like the scent of distant flowers. Maryam opened her eyes, still not fully grasping where she was. She lay there, staring, trying to make sense of what she had experienced. Slowly returning to reality, she sat up in bed. The weight of the real world pressed down on her, forcing her back onto the mortal plane. She stood and tidied herself, then slipped into jeans, pulled on a sweater, and slid her feet into soft Uggs. “How wonderful that they’ve taken care of everything,” she thought gratefully, appreciating the warmth and comfort.

At that moment, there was a knock at the door, and Mikhail appeared in the doorway. His presence always brought with it an atmosphere of warmth and care. He entered, carrying a tray, and smiled that unique smile of his, the one that made her heart feel lighter.

"Thank you very much, Mikhail. Please, have a seat."

He sat on a chair by the table. Looking at him, she involuntarily pondered his unusual appearance: piercing black eyes, a neat short haircut, and slightly pointed ears, all of which gave him the look of an extraordinary person.

"How are you feeling, Maryam?" he broke the silence.

"I have a headache, but in other respects, I'm fine," she admitted.

"Let's fix that now," he said, looking attentively at her forehead. Suddenly, her entire body filled with warmth, as if a hot current ran through her veins. She felt a rush of heat. The headache vanished as if it had never existed, and waves of joy and gratitude filled her being! She looked at him in surprise:

"What was that, Mikhail?"

"This is only a small part of what you can learn, Maryam. This is knowledge. You must work at it, and many things will become accessible to you."

"But how will this help me save my son? When can I go look for him?" Mikhail sighed, as if he had heard the same question for the hundredth time:

"Maryam, you did not fully grasp yesterday's lesson. You are still thinking only of yourself and your son. You need to learn to care for all suffering people. Do you understand?"

She lowered her eyes.

"Yes, you're right. I am selfish".

He smiled:

"Well, acknowledging guilt is already a small victory. For now, you need to stay here; you are not ready yet, and here, you are needed. The children await you!"

"Oh, how shameful, I promised my friends I'd start work early," she realized.

"Don't worry, it's only seven in the morning. You will have time for breakfast and then to work."

"You're right! That's what I'll do." She sat down at the table, said a prayer, and enjoyed her breakfast. "The oatmeal with nuts and dried fruits is wonderful," she said to Mikhail, "and a cup of good black tea, what a morning delight. Thank you so much, Mikhail."

Maryam briefly touched his hands, then dashed outside. The damp, gray morning air hit her face. Her friends greeted her warmly, hugged her, and accompanied her to the children. Seeing Maryam, the little ones rushed toward her with joy. Some ran straight into her knees, some tugged at her sleeve, and the youngest girl held up a drawing:

"This is for you, Aunt Maryam!"

On the sheet, a pencil had drawn a flower with a huge smile. Maryam pressed the drawing to her chest:

"What a beauty! Thank you, sunshine. We'll definitely hang it in the most visible place. Now, let's go, it's time."

Holding hands and chatting happily, they entered the classroom. To her surprise, eight small desks were already neatly arranged in two rows. On each desk were stacks of graph notebooks and lined paper, rulers, writing supplies, pencils, and notepads...

"How did they manage to keep all this?" she wondered, walking around her desk. It was as if they had anticipated the coming events and had prepared everything in advance.

She tested the children and seated them according to their knowledge level, placing the youngest at the front desks near her own. She handed out assignments and sat at her desk, thoughtfully watching the children. *What interesting and educational thing should I tell them*, she pondered, her gaze sweeping over the bowed heads. A quiet voice drew her from her thoughts:

"Aunt Maryam, will there be a fairy tale today?"

"Yes, my dears, there will be. Did you complete all I asked?"

The children nodded and rustled, quickly putting away their notebooks and pencils.

Maryam gathered their work, put it away in the desk, and seated them on the soft mats arranged around her desk.

"Yes!" the children answered in unison.

Maryam collected their work, put it away in the desk, and seated everyone on soft mats around her table.

"Children, you will learn that we are God's creations. And within each of us, there is a part of Him."

"What do you mean?" someone shouted.

"Children, be patient and do not interrupt," Maryam said gently, a smile returning to her lips. She mentally remembered that not long ago, Arizal had told her as a child how important patience was. "Truly, children teach us patience. Only by giving birth to children do we learn this science," she thought and continued... "The Creator made the first human, Adam, from the Earth and breathed life into him. That breath was His part within him."

"And where did He blow to make Adam alive?" asked Yulia, her eyes open wide.

"The Creator breathed into his nostrils, as written in the ancient books. And the man became alive. He was very lonely, watching the animals; they had companions, but man had none. So, he asked the

Creator for a companion, and the Creator heard him. He put Adam to sleep, and when he was asleep, He took a rib from him and made from it a companion, Eve. They lived happily in the Garden of Eden. They had everything, and only one restriction: not to eat the fruit from the tree in the middle of the garden.

That tree is called: the *Tree of Knowledge of Good and Evil.*"

"Why shouldn't they eat from that tree?" asked a little boy sitting nearby. "Did the Creator not want to give them the fruits?" Maryam smiled softly:

"No, my dears," Maryam replied. "The Creator had no shortage of fruits for them. This was simply a kind of task for them. They had to wait a little, until a certain time."

"Perhaps that is patience?" someone asked.

"Exactly! Humans are not born completely perfect. They come into this world to work on themselves. And each has their own work!" "But why must we always work?" asked a nine-year-old boy.

Maryam leaned toward him slightly, as if sharing a secret known only to her:

“You know, I'm going to tell you the story of a letter. A mother wrote it to her son. In it, she explains why we must always work. Not because someone ordered us to, but because it is our nature, our purpose.”

She straightened up, swept her gaze over their attentive faces, and began to tell the story:

LETTER TO MY SON.

Son, our entire life is a struggle — above all, a struggle with ourselves. When we are born, we fight for survival.

It hurts the mother, yes, but the child suffers too. In essence, he dies to his former life — that cozy, protected existence — and is born into a new one. The child, feeding on his mother's milk, struggles again. He must earn that milk; at first, suckling is difficult, but later it becomes a joy for both mother and child. Then comes crawling and walking — another struggle. He must overcome fear. It's terrifying to crawl alone, yet soon it becomes fascinating, because now he can reach what interests him without pleading for his mother's help.

Walking is even scarier. It's a struggle to stand, to find balance, to avoid falling — and when he falls, to rise again, and keep walking. And so, he fights his fear and moves forward. Then comes kindergarten — a new struggle. It's frightening to be among strangers. The

child must learn to trust, to communicate, and to step out of the comfort and safety of home. And then comes school— another trial. New people. Early mornings when he wants to sleep. Long classes when he longs to play.

Homework when he'd rather do anything else. It's a battle against laziness. As he grows, he faces a choice: give in to idleness and drift with the current — or fight, learn, and endure. But those who drift achieve nothing.

They never learn to be born, to crawl, to walk. They never truly become human. After school, another

challenge awaits — university. Again, a choice: study

hard for exams or enjoy life with friends. This, too, is a struggle with oneself. Instead of pleasure, one must force oneself to learn, overcome the fear of teachers, and pass exams. Then comes work. One must present oneself well to be chosen, then wake early every day to go to

work. Sometimes one wants nothing more than to stay in bed and give up. But that, too, is a battle with

laziness. One must rise, pray — for without prayer the day cannot begin — go to work, and deal with people.

One must smile, even when one does not wish to.

Without this effort, there is no growth. Then comes love

— and with it, a new struggle. Two people, each with their own world, share the same space. At first, it's light and easy — laughter, warmth, romance. But soon the real work begins: two almost strangers must learn to become one. And this is hard work — overcoming habits, pride, egoism. Adapting to another person is

never easy. There is no family without effort. It takes years — filled with joy and quarrels, times when you want to leave. Leaving is always easier. But when passions cool, and you listen to the quiet voice within,

you realize many things could have been said or done differently. With each moment of patience, with each difficulty overcome, the bond deepens. Then come children — and again, a struggle.

When the child demands your time while you are exhausted, when you long to rest or see friends, you must overcome yourself and give that time. But when you see the joy in your child's eyes, your heart fills with happiness, and you know — this is what truly matters. Every act of self-overcoming brings pain and resistance. You don't want to do it — but you must. And though it's hard, the reward is immense. After each victory, however small, you grow — in strength, in dignity, in peace.

That is life! It is full of joy and pain, disappointment and happiness — but above all, it is overcoming! Life is work upon oneself. And when we have endured —through all falls and rises — we can be happy at the end, knowing we have not lived in vain. We have completed the work God gave us. Then comes old age— not the worst time, but another stage of inner work.

Something always aches, yet we must go on.

Grandchildren arrive, and now you can give them what you could not give your children — time, patience, understanding. You now have both experience and peace. It is vital to keep an interest in life — to find joy in something: chess, painting, fishing, reading — whatever stirs the soul. For laziness is the true aging.

Laziness brings depression, and depression leads to ruin. Then comes death, which may not be frightening at all if you have worked on yourself and passed through all stages of overcoming. You rejoice, knowing you will soon meet your Creator, and you have no regrets. Death is not the end; it is a transition into another world. If you have lived rightly, there is nothing to fear. Death may come suddenly or slowly, through illness, and even illness is purification. It is given so that you may understand more deeply, so that your heart may open. People, sadly, come closest to God in

suffering, not in joy. But if one realizes what was wrong in life, if one repents sincerely and calls upon God, one will be purified.

Life is beautiful — with all its struggles. And it is vital to remember why we came into this world: to overcome, to grow, to perfect ourselves. To become purer and better — so that God, looking upon us, rejoices!

Maryam fell silent. A special quiet settled over the room, the kind that comes when words are no longer needed — they've already reached deep into the heart.

"So," Artem whispered, "if I make my bed, that's... creativity too?" "Of course," Maryam nodded. "Because you put a piece of yourself into it. You're not just folding a blanket, you're caring for your space, your home. And that is already a little miracle."

"And if I help Mom wash the dishes?" Liya asked, lifting her chin. "That's work too, work that makes the world better. You're not just washing plates, you're keeping the warmth in the house. You're participating in creating harmony."

"So," the boy who had asked the first question thought aloud, "even if I solve a math problem, I'm... creating too?"

"Exactly!" Maryam's eyes lit up again. "You overcome challenges, train your mind, and discover something new. That is your work on yourself. And when you learn something and can help another, that's when your work becomes truly great."

"Now, kids, it's time for lunch," she said with a smile.

"But what about Adam and Eve?! You didn't finish!" the children shouted at once, crowding around her.

"Yes, I remember. And we will continue as soon as we return. But now, wash your hands quickly!" she called cheerfully, tickling them lightly as she sent them to the washbasin.

In the dining room, while the children were eating, a young man of about twenty approached her.

"I need to speak with you.

Urgently," he said quietly, almost in a whisper.

Maryam nodded, gesturing for him to join her at a separate table, but he shook his head:

"Not here. Better if we go outside."

"Quickly, then. I can't leave the children alone," she replied just as quietly.

They stepped outside. The young man introduced himself as Zar and, without looking her in the eyes, blurted out:

"I have information about your son." Maryam's heart clenched painfully.

"What did you say?" she whispered, feeling her voice sink somewhere deep inside.

"Tell me... How is he? Alive?!"

"He's doing fairly well. Overall, he's holding up. They punish him sometimes, but he's correcting himself."

"Punish him?" she asked through tears.

Zar lowered his gaze, as if the words were heavy for him to speak:

"He prays, and they're strict about that. When they catch him praying, they punish him. For several days, he's not allowed to go outside. He's isolated from everyone, sits in a room, and listens to lectures claiming God doesn't exist. But... It's happening less and less. He's improving."

Maryam stared at him silently, unable to utter a word. Her throat tightened, her breath caught. Finally, she whispered, barely audible:

“And what happens next?”

“Next, once they finish ‘working’ with him, he’ll join their army ranks, and possibly rise to the elite. But for that, he must work hard.”

“Work hard? What else must he do?”

“It means to stop spreading the ‘nonsense’ about God. Forget prayer. Stop helping others. Inform on his own brother. Give his earnings with interest... and more. Then he becomes elite, gets a separate room, and eventually a separate home, servants... and women.”

Maryam felt the ground slip away beneath her feet.

“What am I supposed to do? How can I help him?” she asked in a trembling voice.

“For now, stay here. I’ll find you, help you get out of here, and reach the camp. But about our meeting, tell no one,” he said, his gaze piercing and cold.

Something strange flickered in her soul at that look, but she brushed it aside: Not now. He knows about my son.

“Alright, Zar. I won’t tell anyone. If you can... please tell my son, by God’s help, I will find him.”

“Yes, I’ll try,” he called back as he ran off.

Maryam stood for a few more seconds, listening to the fading echo of his footsteps, then slowly turned and headed back to the dining hall. As she crossed the threshold, the children immediately sensed a change. Their cheerful chatter quieted, and curious eyes turned toward her.

"Aunt Maryam, what happened? Why were you crying?" She forced a smile.

"Everything is fine, children. I wasn't crying, just the wind outside that blew some dust into my eyes. And I see you've finished. Well done! Now let's clean up together. Today, Alena will be the eldest on duty. She's eleven. She will wash the dishes, and you will help her."

Maryam spoke as she instinctively assigned tasks: some carried dishes, others wiped the tables, and took out the trash. In half an hour, everything was done, and they returned to the kindergarten. Maryam tucked all the children into their beds and softly sang them a lullaby, "Behind the Stove a Cricket." She had once sung it to her own son, back in those distant days when the world felt simple and kind, when night was just for sleep, not for worries. One by one, the children drifted off to sleep. Maryam sat nearby, listening to their steady breathing.

Her thoughts would not settle:

What should I do? How should I act? Whom can I consult? Should I tell Arizal and Mikhail about this meeting? Something inside tells me they won't like it. And Zar said not to speak about him. Then, not now... she decided, feeling the thought settle like a heavy stone on her chest.

Maryam sighed, dropped to her knees, and whispered:

"Lord, grant me wisdom and strength, show me the right path. Protect my son and everyone near me..."

Outside, the sounds of work filled the air: saws rang, axes struck...

"Time to get the children up."

"Hey, lazybones, get up," Maryam said quietly, approaching them. The children stirred reluctantly, unwilling to wake. Some pulled the blankets over their heads, others squinted, shielding their eyes from the light streaming through the cracks.

"Come on, wake up. We're needed."

Her voice, soft but insistent, gradually cut through their sleepy haze. They fidgeted, and within a few minutes, a lively line of little figures followed her to where the work was in full swing.

The yard was bustling. Men carried materials, women sorted supplies, and the muted chatter and tapping of tools filled the air. Much had already been done, yet plenty remained. They needed to stockpile fuel for the winter, a challenging task. But Hakim had a clever idea. Since the upper parts of many trees were infected, and not all trees were suitable for firewood, he showed how to harvest from the lower part of the trunk, where the wood remained healthy.

Maryam listened with interest as Hakim explained the process, demonstrating how to properly trim branches, leaving only what was needed. They left healthy trees untouched. There was still much work to be done in restoring plants and trees.

"Come on, children," Hakim said with a smile, "you can help me collect the fallen branches. It will be useful, and fun too!"

The children enthusiastically joined in, running around, gathering branches, and laughing whenever someone stumbled. Maryam watched them, her heart filling with warmth. How beautiful these moments were, moments that brought the children together and taught them to work as a team.

Listening to herself, she felt a quiet resolve. The pain from her conversation with Zar had not disappeared, but it receded into the background. *I must be strong—not only for my son, but also for these children, who look at me with such trust and hope.*

CHAPTER 9
DOUBTS

Maryam closed the door behind her and leaned against it, letting the silence envelop her from all sides.

Only then did she feel the depth of her exhaustion—not just physical, but as if everything inside her had been burned to ashes. She removed her scarf, tossed it onto a chair, and sank onto the edge of the bed.

One thought spun endlessly in her mind: What now? How should I act? Zar's face appeared again, his tense gaze, his words that still sent chills through her.

I will find you and help you get out...

But how? When? And most importantly, could she trust him?

Somewhere deep, almost at the edge of consciousness, a thought scratched at her mind: Tell Arizal. It's wrong to stay silent. But immediately, Zar's gaze surfaced—stern, leaving no room for objection: No one must know about our meeting.

A soft knock at the door made her flinch.

"Come in," she said, trying to keep her voice firm.

Mikhail appeared in the doorway. In the dim light of the corridor, his silhouette seemed taller than usual. He stepped inside and closed the door behind him.

"Good evening, Maryam! How was your day?"

“Good evening, Mikhail. Fine. Busy,” she replied briefly. Then, to anticipate further questions, she added, “We cleaned the yard with the children, then Hakim showed them how to properly prepare firewood. The children gathered branches and laughed...”

Mikhail listened silently. Then he tilted his head, as if adjusting not to her words, but to what lay beneath them.

“Maryam,” he said softly, “are you sure there’s nothing more you want to tell me?”

“No... everything’s fine.” She quickly stood. “We’re going to see Arizal, right?”

“Yes,” he replied, letting out a slight sigh. “But first, eat.”

He set a tray of dinner before her.

Avoiding his penetrating gaze, Maryam sat at the table, said a quick prayer, and began eating. When she finished, Mikhail still stood nearby, watching her intently, as if expecting something.

“I’m ready,” she said, faster than necessary.

He nodded and silently led her down the corridor. He stopped at the door to Arizal’s office, knocked, and without waiting for a response, turned and left, leaving her alone.

Maryam found this odd. She paused for a second, trying to calm the trembling in her fingers, then pushed the door open. It creaked softly.

Arizal was seated at his desk, absorbed in reading. Maryam stood for a few seconds, hesitant to break the silence, until he finally lifted his gaze. The heat of his stare coursed through her body, her cheeks flushed, her breath caught. She remained in that state for several seconds.

He exhaled softly.

“Maryam, come in, sit down.”

Swaying slightly, she reached the chair and practically collapsed into it. Arizal stepped closer and took her hand. At his touch, warm waves of trust and care ran through her, her breath evened out, and strength filled her.

“What... was that, Arizal?” “Maryam, you may call me Teacher,” he replied calmly.

“Do you agree to be my student?” She shook her head, confused.

“I don’t know... Forgive me, I don’t understand anything. Who are you? Where do you come from? What do you want from me? Why are you helping me? And are you helping me at all?”

He smiled faintly.

“You have so many questions, Maryam. But most of the answers you already carry within yourself. You only need to learn to listen. Ask your soul: Who am I? And why am I here? — and try to hear what it answers.” “And what if I cannot hear?” she asked softly. “Why can’t you just tell me everything yourself?”

“Everything in its own time, Maryam. We need nothing from you. It is you who needs our knowledge. And we will help you,” he paused and looked at her questioningly, “—if you do not act rashly.”

She lowered her gaze and remained silent.

“Very well, Maryam, let us continue studying. I have already told you that the letters of this alphabet carry immense power. With their help, one can heal and change reality, if it is done for the good, not for personal gain.

You can communicate with us over a distance, using only thought. As soon as you call us, we will hear you. In time, you may even move through space."

Maryam stared at him, speechless.

Everything that was happening seemed incredible, almost unreal.

"Yes, Maryam," he nodded, as if answering her unspoken thoughts.

"All will be given to you if you work diligently."

"How long will it take?" "That depends..."

"On what?"

"On you as well."

"And on what else?"

"If you purify yourself, the Creator will reveal all this knowledge to you. But you will have to wait until you are worthy of the great abundance the Creator has prepared for you in its entirety."

"And if I'm not? I don't have much time."

"Maryam," he said, looking at her with a faint sadness, "there is no time and no space. When will you finally understand this?"

Just as one material object is separated from another by space, so too are spiritual objects separated by the change of form. For example, if two people are united in thought and feeling, no distance can divide them. Conversely, when they differ in opinion and harbor resentment, physical closeness will not bring them together spiritually. Difference of form, difference of viewpoint, that is what creates distance.

Similarity of form, expressed in unity of opinion, brings them together, even if a whole world lies between them. And if the character of one is opposite to the character of another in all respects, they are as far apart as north is from south.

"What does that mean?" she asked. "If I become your like-minded ally, will I more easily purify myself and receive knowledge from you?"

"What does it mean to be our like-minded ally?" she asked barely audibly.

"It means trying to doubt less, to trust more, and to listen to us!" he replied calmly, yet in his voice there was a firmness that sent a shiver down Maryam's spine.

She remained silent, desperately wanting to tell him about Zar, but something inside warned her not to. He would not approve.

Arizal sighed, sensing her inner struggle.

"Doubt is also a blessing," he said more gently. "Because through doubt you grow and reach for knowledge.

By doubting, you search, you explore, you begin to see from different angles and form your own understanding."

"Very well, I hear you, Teacher," Maryam said quietly. "I'm a little tired today. May I go to my room?"

"Of course, Maryam, go," he replied, looking intently into her eyes.

She stepped out, gently closing the door behind her. Arizal remained alone. For several minutes, he sat motionless, then set the book aside and fell into deep thought:

"Still, Maryam must walk this path on her own. Until she separates herself and passes through her trials, she will not understand. Therefore, she must step away from us completely for now, for her qualities are still opposite to ours. I intend to give her knowledge in abundance; from here on, everything depends on her."

CHAPTER 10
THE ESCAPE

That night, Maryam slept restlessly.

She was overwhelmed by nightmares—vague, disturbing, as if someone was watching her from the darkness. At one point, she felt a heavy gaze, piercing and cold. Fear froze her

body. She tried to move—but couldn't.

"Lord... don't leave me..." she whispered in her sleep.

In that instant, the invisible gaze seemed to quiver, sending a wave of energy so strong that Maryam, as if struck by lightning, flew off the bed. She screamed and woke up.

"Lord, what was that?" Trembling all over, Maryam rose from the floor, dressed, and approached the window. Below, in the moonlight, stood Zar.

He was tossing small stones against the glass. She opened the window, and he nimbly climbed into the room.

"Maryam," he said softly. "The time has come. You must go to your son.

He's waiting for you."

"But how?" she whispered, bewildered. "We have nothing—no costumes, no supplies..."

"Don't worry," Zar replied confidently. "I've prepared everything."

“All right,” she said uncertainly and quickly began to get ready: pulling on jeans, a warm sweater, a jacket, a hat, and gloves.

“I’m ready...”

Zar grabbed her hand, giving her no time to think, and helped her climb out the window. “We need to hurry,” he whispered. “It will be dawn soon.”

Multiple thoughts grouped in Maryam’s mind as she struggled to keep up with him. Doubts about the correctness of her actions clashed with the burning desire to see her son.

“Where are we going?” she asked anxiously.

“Maryam, questions later, once we get out of here.”

They reached a wall. Zar whistled softly, and from the other side, someone threw down a rope ladder. He tossed her a bag containing a special suit:

“Change quickly, and don’t forget to put the mask on your face.”

After checking on her, he helped her climb, supporting her from below. Once over the wall, Maryam glanced back. Behind them stretched a scorched, gray field. It looked as if they had stumbled onto the set of a disaster movie.

“I wonder, who threw us that ladder?” she thought.

“Maryam, don’t linger,” Zar called, turning around. Impatience flashed in his eyes. “We can’t waste time.” Maryam shivered at his tone and hurried after him.

As the sun rose over the horizon, an even more terrifying scene extended before them: a dead city, buried under a shroud of white radioactive ash. The further they walked, the grimmer the landscape became. Fear locked her movements, penetrating every cell of her body. The city, once full of life, now only reminded her of the people who had lived there.

Partially destroyed buildings and some completely ruined ones looked like ghosts. Maryam instinctively grabbed Zar's hand. He squeezed hers.

"Don't be afraid..."

Suddenly, a few figures appeared ahead, moving toward them.

"We have a problem!" Zar screamed. "Run!"

They bolted. Maryam's heart pounded as if it might burst out of her chest.

"There's shelter!" he shouted, veering into a narrow alley.

"Phew... looks like we shook them off," Maryam exhaled.

But the relief was short-lived as the alley was through, and six, seven men surrounded them and lunged...

Maryam awoke in a damp, dark room. Her entire body ached. Her head throbbed. With great effort, she lifted herself and sat up.

"Where am I?" she thought, trying to make out anything in the darkness. Her cries for help had no effect.

Silence. Sticky fear began creeping into her heart. "Why am I here, and why is no one coming for me? What are they planning to do with me?"

The door creaked open, and a tall, well-built man appeared in the doorway, his face unseen.

"Woman! Out!" a harsh voice commanded.

Maryam shivered. She struggled to stand on trembling legs and staggered toward the door.

Something caught her foot, and she stumbled, literally flying outside. The bright sun blinded her, keeping her eyes closed.

"Here, take this," the man said, tossing her a mask. She put it on, squinting at the stranger before her. He was nearly a giant, over two meters tall, broad-shouldered, wearing a gray cloak and a mask covering his face.

"Why am I here? Who are you? What do you want from me?" Her words tumbled out, betraying her fear.

"Silence! I ask the questions here."

Maryam bit her lip, trying to calm herself.

"What is your name?"

"Maryam," she answered in a trembling voice.

"How did you get here, and where were you going?"

"I wanted to find my son." "Where is your son?"

"After the explosion, he was taken away. They say—to the camps."

He paused for a moment. Even behind the mask, his gaze seemed to burn through her.

"How did you manage not to get infected?"

"I don't know. All this time, I lived behind the wall."

"Behind the wall?" He laughed roughly. "So, you're from there? From that 'Paradise'? Why did you leave them? Life must be so sweet there.

Everyone's so kind and courteous. They believe in good and evil..." His face flushed crimson, lips trembling. "But there's no good! Where is this good? If it exists, how did He, the one you all speak of, allow this? Where was He when the world crumbled under ash and screams? Where?!

You're silent!? There is no God, and there never was."

He turned abruptly.

"There's only the Chief and his Elite.

Everything else is fairy tales."

Maryam froze, afraid to even breathe. The figure before her gradually seemed to dissolve, more and more like a madman. Suddenly, he stepped toward her.

"Why are you silent? Why aren't you defending Him?"

"And why should I say anything? He is absent from you because you yourselves have turned away from Him. And that is why you live in darkness, where chaos reigns."

"Chaos?!" he laughed. "I'll show you what chaos is."

The man grabbed her hand and dragged her toward a grim structure resembling an ancient Roman atrium. In the center was an arena, surrounded by ten tiers of stone seats. Nearby, under a canopy, were cages with thrashing people.

"Look, foolish woman, this is chaos!" he shouted, signaling his minions. People appeared, and with a clatter, metal shutters inclined around the arena, turning it into a kind of circus ring. In the center, a passage with miniature rails appeared, along which cages were brought into the arena.

"Enough!" he yelled as two cages were brought out.

"And now, all eyes on the stage!" he said with a kind of twisted delight, a glint of anticipation on his face.

The cages creaked open. Emaciated naked people leapt out, their hips wrapped in rags. Dark-skinned, veins bulging on completely bald heads, eyes bloodshot and blazing with a feral, animalistic fire. They froze, scanning the arena with vacant eyes, and suddenly, as if on an invisible signal, attacked one another. No cries, no words—just muffled blows, rasps, the cracking of bones. The sight was monstrous—people literally tore each other apart, biting into throats, gnawing flesh. Two once-human beings now resembled wild beasts.

Blood splattered the gray stone, leaving crimson streaks that seeped into the cracks between the slabs.

The air was thick with a metallic smell, making her head spin. Maryam felt nausea rise in her throat, and her ears rang from the nightmare unfolding before her. She closed her eyes in horror. Lord, help them! Lord, forgive them! she whispered. They do not know what they are doing... Lord, protect us... The man nearby jerked and spun toward her abruptly.

"What are you whispering? Stop!

Watch!" he hissed.

But after that, she could see nothing. First, her head spun, the ground seemed to slip beneath her feet, and then complete darkness swallowed her. She woke up to the smell of dampness and rotting fabric—a musty, nauseating stench that made her want to hold her breath. At least not in that basement, she thought, rising and looking around. The small room had minimal furniture: a bed, a table, and a chair. No windows, no toilet. She knocked on the door.

After a minute, a young man appeared in the doorway, pale, with a tired face, but there was still something human in his eyes, not completely broken.

“What do you want?” he asked.

“Water. I want to drink.” He snorted.

“Drink? We all want to drink here.

This isn’t the city behind the wall, where you’re given food and water. This is reality.”

“Yes, I understand that already,” she replied quietly.

“I’ll ask Dimyon,” he said and left.

Fifteen minutes later, he returned with a metal container of water.

“Drink!” he said, staring at her intently.

Maryam felt uneasy under his gaze.

She removed her mask and whispered a short prayer before taking a sip. The water was warm and stale. I hope I don’t catch cholera, she thought. No choice, I’ll trust God.

Prayer works miracles, she tried to calm herself. The young man left silently, leaving her alone. I wonder where Zar is? Why did he leave me? What if he’s with them? Or maybe he’s being held here too... or worse, maybe he’s already dead? Lord, have mercy. I hope he’s alive. I need to do something. She knocked again. Footsteps approached, and moments later, the same young man stood in the doorway.

“What’s your name?” Maryam asked.

“Why would you care?”

"Sorry, I just don't know how to address you."

He shrugged.

"We don't have names, only numbers. I'm 320."

Maryam looked at him sadly.

"Well, what did your mother call you as a child?"

"Doesn't matter, you don't need to know," he said, hiding his eyes.

Something barely observable, yet still human, flickered across his face at the word mother. Mother is a magical word. It works wonders on the soul, even if a complete scoundrel stands before you.

"Listen, 320, I need to use the toilet.

Please show me the way." "You're not allowed."

"What do you mean, not allowed?

What should I do? Right here?"

He looked at her slyly and let out a crude laugh.

"Why not?"

"All right, fine, as you wish, but you'll have to clean up yourself. I can't leave here."

"Uh-uh, stop making things up.

Come on, let's go. I'll show you, and just this, no nonsense, or I'll get in trouble badly."

"Of course," she agreed, following him while secretly glancing around, looking for the slightest chance to escape.

They walked past half-destroyed buildings. By one of them, she noticed a huge pile of sacks, stacked almost to the top of the fence. If I'm lucky... she thought. The toilet was a little farther off, four metal walls held together by rusty bolts, a roof of intertwined branches, with a piece of old tarpaulin on top. In the corner yawned a pit, emitting a heavy stench.

"Well, here's your throne," he smirked.

"Thank you," Maryam nodded and stepped inside. She held her breath, listening as his footsteps faded. She looked up. Overhead were branches and a tarpaulin. Lord, help me, she whispered. Carefully, trying not to make noise, she pushed aside the branches and lifted the piece of tarpaulin. A streak of light fell across her face. Maryam pulled herself up, grasping the edge of the roof, and began climbing out. The structure proved quite unstable.

Balancing on its wobbling walls, she barely managed to stretch her foot toward the nearest sack, pushed off, and almost fell straight down. At the last moment, she caught the edge and, straining every muscle, climbed over. Her heart was pounding wildly.

Reaching the top, she rolled herself over the fence and got stuck hanging. That was where the real trouble began. On the other side, there were no sacks. Slowly, relying only on her arms, Maryam reached a nearby tree. With fingers trembling from exertion, she grabbed the rough bark and began to climb down carefully. But fate had prepared another trial: the lower branch, rotten through, cracked loudly under her weight, and Maryam fell to the ground. Fortunately, she avoided serious injuries, though a minor sprain seemed certain. Not feeling the pain yet, she broke into a run — not knowing where, just away from that place. Behind her, she heard noise and shouting, then a long, piercing howl.

"Lord..." Maryam whispered as she ran. "Help that poor 320. Let them not punish him too harshly."

CHAPTER 11
A NEW ACQUAINTANCE

No one crossed her path.

"Thank God..." she exhaled, feeling the tension slowly ease. Ahead, a wide field stretched out. Twilight was falling. Maryam glanced anxiously at the horizon: night was approaching, cold and dangerous. "I can't stay here." She prayed and then looked ahead again. On the far side of the field, a small hut came into view.

Maryam cautiously made her way toward it. Upon reaching it, she hid behind a large rock and began to observe. First, an old man emerged from the hut. He surveyed the surroundings, lifted some kind of box, and went back inside. A few minutes later, an elderly woman appeared on the doorstep. She paused, admiring the sunset, sighed, and went back inside as well. Gathering her courage, Maryam stepped out of her hiding spot and knocked on the door. In response — silence. She knocked a little louder.

"Please," she began, "I saw you, and I know you're home. My name is Maryam. I'm looking for my son — he was taken after the catastrophe. I have nowhere to go, and it's too dangerous to stay outside. For God's sake, please let me in!"

After a moment, the door slowly opened, and an elderly woman appeared, with kind but reddened eyes. Maryam instinctively stepped back.

"Don't be afraid, child," the old woman said. "I'm not sick. It's just a little trick we do with the old man — we rub our eyes with onion when there's danger nearby, so no one touches us. They think we're infected."

Maryam smiled.

"That's clever!"

"Come in, child, don't stand on the doorstep — it's dangerous," the old woman said, inviting her inside.

Maryam stepped over the threshold. Inside was a small room. In the corner, a tiny kitchenette, next to it a table and two chairs, an old sofa with two prayer mats on it, and nothing else.

"And where do you sleep?" Maryam asked in surprise.

The woman smiled.

"When it all happened, the old man and I dug a dugout under the house, and that's where we sleep."

She studied her guest carefully, as if deciding whether to trust her. Then she gently took Maryam's hand.

"My name is Zaynab, and this is my husband Khalid. I see, my daughter, you've been through a lot," she said quietly. "Tell me what happened."

Unable to hold back her tears, Maryam began recounting how her life had changed after the calamity, the search for her son, and all the horrors she had endured. Words poured out in a stream she could not stop. The elders listened with sympathy. Zaynab hugged Maryam, holding her close like a mother to a daughter.

"We cannot leave you without help," the old man said. "We have a little food and a place for you to spend the night. But keep in mind, it's not safe here. People are wandering around who don't like strangers."

Soon, a modest dinner appeared on the table: a handful of nuts, a bowl of honey, and some fresh flatbreads.

Maryam looked at the food in surprise.

"Where did you get the honey?"

The old man smiled gently.

"About a month ago, a swarm of wild bees came to us, and we took them in. Now they spoil us with their gift. We don't take everything from them — we share it half and half: for their life, for our joy." Khalid brought a small beehive and carefully opened the lid. Inside, the bees moved peacefully, not trying to fly away. It was as if they had become part of this small world, where care and mutual help reigned.

"Every morning, at sunrise, I take the hive outside," he said tenderly. "And in the evening, when the sky darkens, I bring it back inside. The little bees know exactly when to go to work and when to return home." He stroked the wooden lid of the hive with his palm.

"There is an old prophecy: When the last bee disappears from the Earth, humanity will survive for only four more years."

He paused for a moment, then added:

"Do you see, daughter, the bee is one of the most important creatures for the world. Without bees, there will be no pollination. Without plants, there will be no animals. And without them, humans cannot survive.

Everything is connected; everything relies on balance."

He paused for a moment, then spoke quietly, as if reciting from memory:

"Go to the bee and learn how diligent it is, what honorable work it does; its labors serve both kings and commoners; it is loved by all and renowned; though weak in strength, it is honored in wisdom."

"Do you see how important these little creatures are?" the old man said with admiration.

He then took his prayer mat, laid it facing east, and prayed to the Almighty.

"Amen," said Zaynab, spreading a mat for Maryam in the dugout. In the kitchen, under a mat, was a hidden hatch. She opened it and invited Maryam to follow. The old man followed and carefully closed the hatch. Everything was thought out: the mat covered the hatch perfectly, hiding it from unwanted visitors.

Downstairs, Zaynab lit an oil lamp. It smoked a little but provided enough light. Maryam saw the clay room, with niches in the walls serving as beds—two neatly made and the third empty. The elders, wiping away tears, told her that after the explosion, their son was infected and disappeared; nothing has been known about him since. Zaynab spread a bed for Maryam, her son's bed. Settling on it, Maryam's thoughts returned to her son and how to reach him. "God, everything is so difficult. I can't do this alone. And where is Zar?" she thought, quietly sobbing.

"What troubles you, my daughter?" Khalid asked gently.

"I'm sorry, I didn't mean to wake you."

"You did not wake us. The elderly are very light sleepers."

"I keep thinking of my son. How can I save him?"

"Listen, it won't be easy to reach him, but you will succeed. Remember: only a pure, motherly heart, burning with love for God, can enter there and rescue a child from the claws of the Black Dragon."

"A dragon?!" Maryam exclaimed in surprise.

"Yes, a dragon. There is no other way to call him. He is a dark ruler who manipulates people through their weaknesses. Therefore, before you go there, you must purify yourself."

"That's what Arizal told me," she sighed.

"Who is Arizal?" the old man asked. Maryam told them all about her life beyond the high fence. Khalid listened attentively, without interrupting, then let out a sigh:

"Ah... you shouldn't have listened to Zar's temptation. You weren't ready yet. There, they could have helped you. But apparently, you must take your own path. And what is it—you will discover along the way.

"Our life is a chain of decisions, small, insignificant decisions... Each decision places you before a new choice. Sometimes that choice changes everything, and every minute of your life depends on it... You have made a decision and chosen your path. Now you must prepare for the meeting with the enemy." The old man paused for a moment, as if listening to something unseen, and then continued:

The Almighty sees all, knows all, and nothing is hidden from Him. We worship Him and ask for His help! Let Him guide us on the straight path, the path He has blessed. But He does not guide those under His wrath, nor the lost. Those who believe in what has been sent to them must follow it. And they will reach their Lord and succeed.

The evildoers who do not believe—whether you beg them or not—they will not believe. The Almighty has sealed their hearts and ears; a veil covers their eyes. This is a great punishment for them!

Among people are those who say: 'We believe in the Almighty!' But only their tongue speaks; their hearts are silent. They try to deceive the Almighty and those who truly believe, but they only deceive themselves, unaware of the harm their hypocrisy does to their souls. Their hearts are sick. The Almighty will increase their disease! Let them suffer punishment for their hypocrisy. Through it, they spread lawlessness. Truly, these fools do not know what they do!'

"Believe, Maryam, with all your passionate heart. Lift your prayers to the Almighty, ask for people on Earth, and remember: 'A mother's prayer can reach the bottom of the sea.'"

He smiled faintly.

"Now sleep. The Almighty is with us."

Maryam only nodded. Her eyes were already closing when, suddenly, heavy footsteps and muffled voices sounded from above. Khalid pressed a finger to his lips, covered the lamp with a shade so it wouldn't smoke, and sank to his knees, turning his face toward the east. Zaynab, like a shadow, stood beside him and did the same.

Maryam, without hesitation, followed their example.

From above, loud voices shouted:

"She couldn't have gone far! We must find her before the others do!"

"Are you sure she's the one?" another voice asked.

"Yes. That's what Zar said. And he's from the Elite. He knows."

“Tell me, Dimyon, what’s so special about her? A woman is a woman — how is she different from the others?” “You, idiot, who knows nothing about such matters, had better not stick your nose where it doesn’t belong.

Otherwise, it might get torn off,” he cackled.

“Got it, sorry. But as far as I know, those old folks are infected. And she wouldn’t have survived here. They aren’t home now either — must’ve gone hunting.”

“Good point. Let’s get out of here. Dawn is coming, and we still haven’t found her.”

Silence fell. Zaynab rose from her knees and whispered, “A hard day awaits us. We need to sleep a little more.”

Soon, Maryam heard the quiet, rhythmic breathing of the old couple. And soothed by those gentle sounds, she tried to fall asleep. But her agitated mind stubbornly refused to obey. It excitedly tried to understand: what was so special about her, and what did they all want from her?

Yes, since childhood, I have had a remarkable intuition. I have always been able to read people well and predict their actions. But could that really be the reason for such attention?

Sometimes strange images arose in my mind, and later they would come to life. These visions appeared at the most unexpected moments: in dreams, during walks, when I was deep in thought. At first, I considered them simple fantasies, but over time, I began to realize that something more was hidden behind them.

All these years, I had been searching for answers to my inner questions. I remember predicting trouble for a friend and managing to prevent it. Another time, while playing with my son on the playground, I predicted that he would fall and get hurt. At that very moment, I grabbed him by the hand, and he avoided injury. And there were many such situations in my life. But I never gave them any special significance.

Faith in God has always been the most important thing for me. Since early childhood, I knew Him, loved Him, and sought Him in everything. When I was a child, I related to Him as a friend; as an adult, as a father, as the source of life. Just as a flower cannot live without sun and water, I could not live without God's Light.

So, what special abilities are they talking about? If I have them, I never pay attention to them. If it is the Creator's will, He Himself will reveal to me what I need.

"Lord, help me! Reveal to me the meaning of what is happening," she pleaded.

"Lord, I beg You, do not let me make a mistake! Guide my thoughts and actions, be my shield and protector against enemies.

Guard me from dark forces and their temptations; do not let them defile my soul. Help me save my son!"

The words of prayer gradually lulled her, and she sank into a deep sleep. She woke up before the first rays of dawn. In the dim light, she noticed Khalid, who was kneeling on the prayer rug, immersed in prayer.

When he finished, Maryam could not hold back her question:

"Why do you pray so often?" When he turned and looked at her, such wisdom shone through his eyes! "My ancestors did so, and so do I.

The Almighty commanded us to pray five times a day — so that the heart does not fall asleep and the soul does not harden. And why did you wake up so early?"

"I don't know... I couldn't sleep." She also performed her prayer, washed with cool water from the jug, and went upstairs. The house already smelled of smoke, something warm and appetizing. Zaynab was working in the kitchen — moving skillfully between the hearth and the table, quietly humming to herself.

"Good morning," said Maryam, and hurried to help. Together they prepared a simple breakfast: honey, nuts, and oatmeal cooked in water.

Then Zaynab brought out a bowl of flour.

"Where did you get flour?" Maryam asked in surprise.

The old woman smiled mysteriously.

"You'll see a miracle now," she said, and began kneading the dough: mixing flour with water, adding salt, a little honey, and a handful of oats. She shaped flatbreads and laid them on a dry clay pan. Soon, the aroma of fresh bread filled the house. When they sat down to eat the flatbreads with honey, washing them down with a chaga infusion, Maryam could no longer contain herself:

"Tell me, Zaynab... How did you manage to preserve the flour?"

Mischievous sparks glimmered in the old woman's eyes:

"Oh... daughter... this flour is not ordinary. It's wood flour."

"Wood flour?" Maryam raised her eyebrows in surprise.

"Is that even possible?"

Zaynab put the cup aside and sat down next to her, preparing to explain this ancient method passed down through generations.

"In times of famine," she began, "our ancestors used only what they had at hand. The forest provided everything necessary."

"To make wood flour, we use the heartwood of certain trees. We gather twigs and bark, then dry them in the sun, and grind them. It turns into something like flour."

Maryam listened with interest, imagining how their ancestors, as they went into the forest, found sources of food even when it seemed that everything had dried up.

"True," Zaynab continued, "this flour is not as nutritious as grain flour, but it helps satisfy hunger in difficult times. Of course, the taste is a bit unusual, but it's edible."

"Especially with honey," Maryam added with a smile.

The old woman's story touched her deeply. How hard life must have been for their ancestors! And how they used their knowledge and wisdom, even in the darkest times, giving hope that all was not lost, and that wisdom passed down from generation to generation would help humanity survive.

After the meal, they offered a prayer of gratitude to the Almighty together.

"Now, to work," said Khalid, rising. "We need to gather firewood and go to the swamp."

"Why do we need that?" asked Maryam.

"We've eaten, so we must share with the unfortunate — those like us," he replied calmly.

Maryam looked at him in surprise. "Are there really... people? Normal

people, I mean." Khalid nodded.

"Yes, Maryam, there are. If you noticed, we are now outside, without masks."

"Oh, it's true..." she exclaimed. "But how can that be?"

"The thing is," the old man explained, "this virus only affects low souls."

"What does that mean?"

"If a person's soul sought God, had the desire to help others, and be useful to society, such a body, having such a soul, would not be infected. But those who lived only for themselves, indulged in vices, fed on malice and fear — their souls darkened. And when the trial came, these souls could not endure. They burned from the inside, and their bodies turned into wild, merciless beasts."

Maryam listened, holding her breath.

"So, the virus is not a disease, but a purification?"

"You could put it that way," the old man said quietly. "Purification through pain. A trial for the world, to separate the living from the spiritually dead."

"Ah, where is our son now," sighed Zaynab. "May the Almighty help him." "Amen," the old man replied, and after a pause, added:

"Well, enough sitting around, it's time to work. We need to find healthy trees."

"But how will we know which ones are healthy?" Maryam asked.

Khalid smirked slightly:

"You know, back when the world was still as I knew it, I read an article about Hiroshima and Nagasaki. It said that at the moment of the explosion, no living organism could have survived. However, in the park near the Hankawa River, you can see a weeping willow that was planted before World War II. The willow's trunk couldn't withstand the powerful shockwave and broke. Yet, the tree didn't die and continues to sprout. Most of its branches grew and became full-fledged limbs. Just like the weeping willow, many other surviving trees were seriously damaged by the shockwave and the subsequent fire. But that didn't stop them from surviving to this day. The most interesting part is that the explosion destroyed many houses near these trees. But how did the trees survive? Despite their damaged crowns and branches, their trunks remained at least partially intact. As for the high temperature, the bark and moisture helped them endure. Most likely, the outer bark was burned, but the trees themselves didn't die. And what about radiation, you might ask? After all, the trees were exposed to high doses of radiation from the atomic bomb, and radioactive fallout fell on them. The secret is that they are more radiation-resistant than humans or animals. For example, the most resilient trees, such as poplars, can withstand high levels of radiation without problems. Oaks, unfortunately, are better off growing further away, in cleaner areas; we need their acorns.

We collect them and make flour. The technology here is simple: we take slightly unripe acorns, still dark green, and put them in a kind of oven. If you look behind the house, you will see that we dug a round pit, lined it with clay, and placed a metal grate on top. When the fire dies down, we put the acorns in and remove them once their 'shells' start to crack. Then we clean the acorns by hand and grind them in a mortar."

He took a handful of dark flour from a bag and showed it to Maryam.

"Look. The acorn flour is dark. In the past, people who ate bread made from this flour had brown or even black teeth — but they were full and alive. This method was invented in ancient times. Even when there was no grain, humans found a way not to die of hunger."

"And why do we need to go to the swamp?" Maryam asked.

"In the swamp, we need the rhizomes of marsh plants, especially Menyanthes trifoliata. Late in autumn or early spring, when the roots have accumulated nutrients, they are washed, dried in the sun and in an oven, and then ground into flour. This flour is soaked in hot water, allowed to settle, the water is drained, the flour is dried, and then soaked again in hot water to remove bitterness and harmful substances."

"And you can also find uninfected frogs there," Zaynab added with a smile.

"You know so much," Maryam said in awe.

"Live with us for a while, and you'll learn," the old man laughed.

CHAPTER 12
HEALING.
THE PATH OF THE SUFI

Before heading to the swamp, Khalid ordered them to put on protective suits and masks.

"Those mosquitoes are surprisingly resilient and can carry all sorts of infections," he explained. "It's not worth taking the risk."

For about half an hour, the travelers walked in silence. Maryam anxiously glanced around, looking at the swamp shrouded in a misty haze. The foul-smelling reeds and duckweed created an eerie scene.

"Don't forget, watch your step," Khalid reminded them. "The swamp can be deceptive, just like its inhabitants."

Zaynab, staring at the grim waters, suddenly felt an inexplicable unease. Trying to hide her state, she focused on finding the Menyanthes trifoliata, pretending to be fully absorbed in the task.

"There it is!" she exclaimed, pointing to something green breaking through the murky water. Khalid, glancing around cautiously, nodded.

They began their work, carefully extracting the roots from the muddy bottom. But soon their tense labor was interrupted by a splash of water and rustling in the reeds.

"What was that?" Maryam whispered, feeling a chill run down her spine.

"Probably frogs," Khalid answered uncertainly, straining to see in that direction. "We must be careful," the old man said quietly, gripping his shovel tightly as he moved deeper into the reeds. Suddenly, he screamed. Maryam and Zaynab rushed to him. In the thick vegetation, amidst the sticky mud, they saw a human body. He lay face down, covered with dozens of enormous frogs. His skin was gray-green, and his clothes were in tatters. Approaching carefully, they turned him over and cleared the mud from his face. Zaynab let out a stifled cry, and Khalid froze as if rooted to the spot. Maryam leaned closer and studied his features, and her heart stopped.

"320..." she breathed, barely audibly.

Zaynab dropped to her knees beside him and bitterly wept, pressing his cold hand to her chest.

"Son! This is our little boy, Ahmed." Khalid quickly checked his pulse — there was life, though faint, still lingering in his body. "We need to hurry," he said, glancing around. "There could be unwanted guests here." Together, the three lifted his limp body and carried him home. The way back was not easy. Despite the young man's slight frame, every step was a struggle. They had to stop frequently to catch their breath. Upon reaching the house, they closed the doors and lowered him into the dugout. When he was carefully undressed, it became clear that his body was covered with widespread abrasions and bruises.

"Yes, he suffered a lot," the old man said grimly. "Apparently, they decided he was already dead and threw him into the swamp to be torn apart by wild animals and people."

Maryam felt a sharp pain in her heart.

"This is my fault," she cried. "It's all my fault."

"Child, what are you talking about?

How can you be to blame for what happened to our son?" Zaynab asked.

The woman told them everything about their encounter and what had happened. The elders exchanged glances and let out heavy sighs.

"There's no blame on you here," Khalid said. "He chose his path himself. The Almighty only showed him the consequences of serving those devils. But don't worry, with God's help, we'll pull him from the jaws of death."

Maryam cautiously touched his head. The young man looked no older than twenty, though his emaciated appearance and deep shadows under his eyes betrayed a hard life.

Suddenly, she felt intense heat in her palm and a slight tingling. Maryam instinctively pulled her hand back.

"What's wrong, child?" Khalid asked, watching her closely. Maryam explained what had happened.

"Now, try placing your hand on his head again and mentally call upon the Almighty!"

Maryam obeyed. Ahmed stirred.

She continued to hold his head in her hand, feeling the energy flow into the young man, and tried to pour as much love as she could into it.

The young man opened his eyes, and Maryam, exhausted, lost consciousness. When she came to, Ahmed was half-sitting on his bed, and Maryam was lying on Zaynab's bench.

"Forgive me," she said. "With everything that's happened to your son, I've only added more trouble."

"My child, don't speak like that.

Thanks to you, our son woke up," the old woman said, stroking her head.

"Thanks to me, he ended up there," Maryam muttered.

"No," Khalid objected. "He ended up there because of his deeds. But he woke up thanks to you. And, most importantly, by the will of the Almighty." He sighed and added more softly, "Enough talk. Everyone is awake, and praise be to God. You need strength. Eat and rest."

Zaynab made them a healing drink with herbs, cranberries, and honey. They drank it, ate a piece of flatbread, and fell asleep again.

"What a strong girl she turned out to be," Zaynab whispered, addressing Khalid.

Khalid thoughtfully stroked his beard. "Yes, her strength is limitless. She just hasn't learned to control it yet. If she develops her potential, she could become an excellent Warrior of Light."

The old woman stepped closer and looked at the sleeping woman with maternal care.

"But this path is not easy. She will have to go through trials that test not only her body but her soul. Help her with this."

"Alright," he nodded thoughtfully. "For now, let's not disturb her. Let her gather her strength."

Meanwhile, Maryam's consciousness traveled through a wondrous world:

Celestial beings descended from the sky, took her hands, and led her to giant glowing jelly-like masses. "Place your hand there," unspoken voices instructed in her mind. They communicated mentally rather than verbally. Maryam obediently placed her palm in the glowing mass. "Look," in her mind's eye, her entire life flashed before her, like a silent, accelerated film. "Strange," said the beings. "We do not hear you. You possess great power. Look." She saw a fiery-black angel descending from the sky, arms and legs crossed, carrying malice. "Many of us, taking human form, are on Earth to help you," their consciousness conveyed.

Maryam awoke, heart racing.

Maryam woke up abruptly. Her heart was pounding wildly, as if after a long run, and her whole body was trembling.

"What's wrong, my daughter?" Zaynab asked anxiously, leaning over her.

Still shaken, Maryam recounted the strange dream.

"Perhaps the Warriors of Light are knocking at your door," the old woman replied thoughtfully, stroking her hand.

"And who was that fiery black angel?"

"I don't know, maybe a dragon." "You always talk about a dragon.

Does it really exist? Is it not a metaphor?"

"Both yes and no," Zaynab said thoughtfully, lowering her gaze. "The dragon is the evil that rules the Earth now. It is both a dragon and not a dragon. A form, a symbol, an essence... All at once."

"And who are the Warriors of Light?"

"In the Book of Revelation by John the Theologian, known as the Apocalypse, there is a chapter dedicated to the prophecy of the 144 thousand of Warriors of Light, who, once awakened, will change the world, cleanse the Earth of the 'forces of darkness,' evil, and despair, ushering in the Golden Age of Truth, Purity, and Enlightenment. Right now, we live in an era lacking true values, justice, mercy, spirituality — an era dominated by dark energies that breed greed, ignorance, selfishness, lust, hypocrisy, evil, and violence...

And so, the Warriors of Light awaken. It is precisely now, during this period, that the unique opportunity arises to restore one's connection with the Universe, to attempt to bring harmony back into life. That is why, in this utter darkness, the Warriors of Light appear — the Great Teachers and Guides. They do not descend from the heavens in a chariot with a shining sword in hand like Archangel Mikhail. Their only weapons against the 'forces of darkness' are love, patience, and justice, and their main goal is to destroy the darkness within us and show the right path."

Zaynab fell silent, her eyes misted over with memories.

"Unfortunately, our son Ahmed has lost his connection with the Almighty," Zaynab said sadly. "Seduced by the charms of the dark elite, he was tempted by their promises of worldly wealth, rejecting the simple life in our earthen shelter. Three months have passed since that terrible day."

"How?" Maryam asked in horror. "I thought it had been no more than a month and a half..."

"Time has accelerated, Maryam," Zaynab whispered. "We do not notice how it flies. Like sand slipping through our fingers — there was just a handful, and now it's gone."

"How can that be? It was just December."

"Yes," the old woman said with a bitter smile, "and now it's March.

How do you think we could have dug the roots in the swamp in January?"

"But what about winter and the January cold?" Maryam insisted.

"Unfortunately, even the seasons have changed. Everything in the world is disrupted; everything has changed."

"And my son?" she swallowed, trying to hold back tears. "He's been there with them for three months. I need to go there. And as soon as possible."

"Yes, my daughter, you may set out on your journey tomorrow."

"But why tomorrow? Why not today?"

"Today, Khalid will help you understand your power. Without that, you won't be able to endure."

She wanted to argue, but then Ahmed woke up and, seeing Maryam, growled:

"You?! This is all because of you!

They almost killed me."

Zaynab quickly approached him, gently touching his shoulder.

"Son, calm down, quiet! She saved you."

"Saved?! I ended up in this mess because of her," he snapped.

"Son, don't speak like that," his father said sternly. "This woman pulled you out from the very jaws of death."

"Yes, and she almost sent me back there," he muttered.

"Back there? You sent yourself when you went to them," Khalid replied calmly.

"They found me, healed me, and I stayed to work with them..." the young man said bitterly, clenching his fists.

"No, son," his father shook his head. "You're alive because the spark of light remained in you, and your mother's prayer healed you. Not them."

"Father, you didn't see the state they found me in. I was worse than a wild beast."

"Yes," Khalid said softly. "Your physical body only reflected the suffering of your soul, tortured by selfishness. You always craved glory, wealth, and power... Having such desires isn't bad. But remember, true power lies in intention. Not just to take, but also to give."

"What do you mean, Father?" Ahmed asked irritably, glancing at him from under his eyebrows.

"Intention, my son," Khalid replied calmly.

"For example, if you want to earn a certain sum, think not only of yourself but also of how you can help others with that money. When your intentions are pure and your heart is open, the Almighty will guide you where you need to go. Then you will achieve far more than with this so-called Elite."

"Father, you just don't understand.

The Elite — that's everything!!!"

"Yes, I see your 'everything,'" Khalid said wearily. "They beat you like a dog and threw you into the swamp."

"It's all because of her," he said, pointing toward Maryam.

"Tell me, son," Zaynab intervened gently, "what would you want? For them to take her? Where is your humanity, compassion, the desire to help your neighbor?"

"There is none of that!" Ahmed shouted and tried to jump up, but he couldn't; his head spun, and he collapsed back down.

Maryam ran to him, carefully lifted his head, and stroked it. Now she could control the power emanating from her and sense when to give more and when less. Moreover, she saw around his physical form, like a haze, flashes of color — some darker, some lighter, and near his head and chest, almost black.

Maryam remained focused and tried to eliminate the darkness, gradually transforming it into a pure light-blue aura. And she succeeded. She stood up, swayed, and fell. Zaynab ran to her, and together with Khalid, they laid her on the bed. Fifteen minutes later, Maryam regained consciousness.

"Well, here you are with us," Khalid smiled. "Praise be to the Almighty." He sat down beside her and took her hands in his. "Listen, my daughter, there are three forms of culture.

The first is worldly: the simple accumulation of information.

The second is religious: living by established rules. But there is a third: the culture of the chosen — self-development."

He paused.

"The famous Khajveri, the great Sufi Master, said this. Sufis divide the dedicated Teachers of humanity into three kinds: Masters, Prophets, and Saints.

Masters are warrior-teachers. They lead the army of the enlightened, which is obligated to fight against the forces of darkness.

Saints are comforters, intercessors, peacemakers — gentle beings carrying the mission of love and forgiveness.

Prophets are the guardians of the 'Middle Path,' the 'Third Force.' In them, like in an alchemical laboratory, transmutation and reconciliation of contradictions occur, which they surrender themselves to.

They are Teachers, preserving and developing knowledge, messengers of God's Will. Through them, the far-

God's designs are revealed; they are full of insights, sometimes unclear even to themselves. A Prophet is an enlightened Educator who teaches knowledge and experience. He is responsible for the program of global enlightenment, being both Teacher and Student simultaneously. He demonstrates that Knowledge is only partly true, and the path of teaching leads to inner understanding, which is the continuous grasp of the designs of the Divine Mind."

Khalid looked at Maryam attentively and gently. "I know what I'm saying is difficult," he smiled, "but I must initiate you into all of this, as you have a very challenging path ahead. Every person who realizes themselves can find any of these three paths within and choose the one that will reveal their potential."

He paused, then continued: "Divine Love and Truth cannot be harmed or protected. Whoever has felt the presence or touch of God even once does not need proof, nor must they prove anything to others. Sufis remain fully in the earthly world while maintaining a constant connection with the non-earthly. We are not magicians or mystics; we are those who refine people, preparing them to receive the Light."

Maryam thought for a moment. "Then why didn't it work with Ahmed, your son?"

He sighed. "Because our correction in this world is not yet complete, and we must go through this trial together with him. Such is the Will of the Almighty!"

Khalid stood and gestured to the mat in front of him.

"Maryam, sit, close your eyes, and imagine that you are a small flame in the darkness, floating in the air. All of your being is drawn to the fiery river from which you were born. Try to see it and reach for it with your whole soul, touch it, absorb its power..."

"Look for it..."

"I'm looking for it!"

"No, it's not working. Sorry, thoughts about my son keep coming, and I can't think of anything else."

"It's okay, don't worry. You'll manage. Rest, and we'll try again. Here, child, drink this herbal infusion with honey," Zaynab said, stroking her head.

Maryam took a sip; the taste was slightly astringent but very pleasant. She drank it all and fell asleep. In her dream, she kept searching for the fiery river. Suddenly, ahead, she saw a stream of fire. Her whole being was drawn toward it.

When her hands touched the stream, such bliss filled her entire being that no words in this world could describe it. She absorbed the flow into herself, filling her inner reservoir. Until she heard a voice deep within her consciousness:

"Maryam, stop. That's enough. You are ready."

She shot out of the dream as if propelled by a powerful force, breathing heavily, and looked around. Khalid was sitting nearby, smiling.

"Well done, girl, you did it!"

Not understanding, she just blinked at him.

"Now, come to yourself, it's time to get ready."

"Get ready? But it's nighttime!" "No, my dear," Khalid laughed softly, "you slept from yesterday's

lunch until this morning!"

"Oh... how did that happen?"

"It's normal. Your body adapted to the knowledge you absorbed. That always happens."

"And your son? Where is he?"

"He's fine. Thanks to you, he is fully healed. Thank you."

Maryam stood up, her head slightly throbbing, but she felt wonderful overall. She went out into the courtyard and saw Ahmed there, helping his mother tend to the stove. When she approached them, the young man straightened up, his face brightened, and his eyes smiled.

"Hello, Maryam! How are you feeling?"

"Thank you, Ahmed. I feel wonderful. And you?"

"Finally, I heard silence! Thank you, Maryam!"

"Silence is beautiful, for it is the greatest luxury. One can hear God only in silence. And I am very glad that a dialogue with God has opened within you! Now everything here will be fine, despite the surrounding world. I'm truly happy for you."

"The darkest hour is nearest the dawn," Zaynab remarked.

"Come, my children, breakfast time has come, and then we must prepare Maryam for her journey."

At breakfast, Ahmed told Maryam what awaited her when meeting representatives of the Elite.

"I myself have never met the Elite, only their representatives. The most important of these adepts is Zar. He looks very young, but in fact, he is about forty. He is utterly ruthless and possesses immense knowledge.

Above Zar is only the Elite. But Zar already has one foot with them; they need him here among the bee-agents."

He paused, looking aside. "There are worker bees — these are all the people who work for them, ordinary people. They are considered slaves.

Then there are servant bees, who serve the bee-agents.

And the bee-agents — they are like Dimyon. Zar oversees them. Why they need you, I don't know. But I know one thing: you are a very valuable asset. The Elite itself needs you."

"Oh, excuse me, Maryam, I switched to 'you'!"

"It's okay, Ahmed, I'm much more comfortable this way. What a cunning traitor Zar is. How cleverly he lured me out of there. But on the other hand... I still have to get to them; I must take my son," she sighed.

"Maryam, remember one thing," Khalid said, looking her straight in the eyes. "No matter how great the evil you face, you must bless it, but never hate it. Only then will you manage with them. Remember: they have fallen low, and the Light is closed to them. You can only pity them — the doors before them are closed, and they can no longer draw energy from the Divine Flow. And when they cause you pain, your task is to pray for them. Then they will not be able to access you; you will be closed to them. But if anger or hatred awakens in you, the doors will open slightly, and darkness will gain access. Be careful, pray constantly.

May the Almighty protect you on your path!"

Maryam approached the elder and bowed low.

"May the Almighty always protect you."

"Amen!" Zaynab whispered. She packed Maryam's backpack with provisions, added a few personal items, and advised her to wear a special outfit to avoid unnecessary attention. Before leaving, they all prayed together. The silence was filled with their breathing and the murmur of prayers.

Maryam took a deep breath and stepped forward.

CHAPTER 13
THE "BEAST'S" LAIR

Khalid had told her to go east—and so she set off in that direction.

The path led through deserted lands, lifeless and mute. To keep her mind occupied and not surrender to the oppressive weight of dread, Maryam began composing short reflections in her thoughts about the word east.

East—the place where the day is born.

East—the direction of prayer.

East—the path Khalid had shown her.

How many meanings can a single word contain?

She remembered how, from childhood, she had learned to determine the cardinal directions by the sun. Now that skill proved more valuable than ever. Simple truths surfaced in her memory:

The sun rises in the east and sets in the west.

If you stand with your arms outstretched—your right hand pointing toward the rising sun and your left toward the setting—then north lies ahead of you and south behind.

And when the sun reaches its zenith, shadows grow shortest. At that moment, the sun points strictly south; north remains behind, with west and east on either side.

Well then, I'll navigate, she thought, walking through the barren land.

Thank God, no one had crossed her path so far. In her pocket lay an onion—just in case she might need to pretend she was infected. Wary of unwanted encounters, she scanned her surroundings constantly. Around her, there was nothing but lifeless earth. Only the wind chased dust along the road.

She walked and did not cease praying. Again and again her thoughts returned to those she had left behind.

How are Arizal and Mikhail? What did they think when they learned I was gone? And the children—little Yulia, my friends... have they forgiven me?

Suddenly, somewhere very close, the roar of an engine erupted. Her heart plunged. Maryam threw herself to the ground and pressed her whole body against the earth.

Lord, I beg You—let them not see me, she prayed.

And a miracle happened: the truck sped past, raising a cloud of dust. Dry earth showered her face, but she did not move until the noise faded completely. Only then did she whisper,

"Thank God..."

The road led her to a scorched field. The ground was blackened, as though coated in charcoal. With great effort—overcoming fear and the nausea rising in her throat—Maryam stepped onto it, weaving her way around lifeless human bodies. The air was thick with the suffocating stench of decay.

Here and there, she saw people who were still alive, but utterly emaciated. Their eyes burned with a hungry gleam, yet they lacked the strength to rise and attack.

Poor creatures, Maryam thought. Hunger has turned them into beings willing to do anything for a scrap of food.

“Forgive them, Lord,” she whispered. “It is not their fault they have become this way.”

Ahead, silhouettes appeared—a man and a woman with a child in her arms.

Their withered bodies were barely covered with rags, and in their eyes burned such hungry despair that Maryam felt her blood freeze in her veins. She understood instantly: these people were ready for anything for food, and she could become their next victim. Perhaps lunch or dinner.

Whatever time it is for them, Maryam thought with a nervous, bitter smile — and ran with all her might, praying silently for the salvation of these unfortunate souls. To her astonishment, the pursuers turned out to be surprisingly fast — hunger had not weakened them, but instead had given them strength. Maryam barely managed to keep the distance. Lord! she gasped. I’m ready to give them everything I have... but would that stop them? In desperation, she threw her pouch of food to them. The woman with the child stopped, but the man would not retreat. He chased her all the way to the road until a truck appeared, driving toward them. Realizing the danger, the man dropped to the ground.

Maryam took the chance — she ran to the vehicle and, when it drew level with her, grabbed the edge and leapt into the back, hiding behind a rough gray curtain. Her heart pounded madly, ready to burst from her chest. God, look at people, they should have come to this!... Forgive us, she whispered with a nervous smile. I almost became someone's dinner just now. I wonder where this truck is headed? She carefully peeked through a gap in the tarp. Ahead loomed massive gates surrounded by a high fence crowned with barbed wire. Oh... have I jumped from the frying pan into the fire? Running is useless — guards are everywhere. They'll notice me anyway... She pressed herself into the corner of the truck bed as the vehicle kept moving, weaving through the compound. Suddenly, the truck stopped. Fear gripped her body when the curtain was abruptly thrown aside, and a voice rang out:

Well, what a surprise!" the man standing by the truck exclaimed with undisguised admiration.

"Well then—come out, since you've come to us of your own accord."

Maryam stepped out. The sun blinded her for a moment, forcing her to squeeze her eyes shut. When her vision cleared, she saw a man of about forty-five standing before her—tall, broad-shouldered, with an almost aristocratic posture and a face where calm bordered on authority.

"You may remove the mask. You won't need it anymore," he said in a steady, confident voice.

Maryam obediently took off the mask.

"Well..." the man drawled, studying her closely. "We've nearly worn ourselves out searching for you. And it turns out you decided to come to us on your own."

His penetrating gaze seemed to reach straight into her soul, making her heart beat faster. A chill spread through Maryam at the powerful energy emanating from him. She lowered her eyes and began to pray silently. The man flinched almost imperceptibly, as if disturbed by a sharp sound, but immediately smiled again.

"My name is Saman. And you..."—he paused theatrically, "Let me think... Maryam, is it not?" He gifted her with a captivating smile.

"I imagine you are tired. Come, let us go inside."

As if in a dream, Maryam followed him obediently. Before her stretched a large, single-story house surrounded by a small garden; beyond a stone arch lay an inner courtyard where an artificial stream murmured, a strange island of calm in the midst of a ruined world.

Crossing the threshold, she was struck by the refined taste of the house's owner. Every detail of the interior spoke of wealth and sophistication.

How did they manage to recreate the atmosphere of the past in such conditions?

Everything in the house breathed luxury: a spacious, welcoming entryway, a tastefully furnished living room, antique paintings on the walls—most likely originals—soft sofas and carpets that created an aura of comfort.

Incredible... such luxury in a world like this.

There must be a few underground levels as well, Maryam thought. That's how everything is built now.

"Why are you standing there?" Saman said with a faint smirk. "Come in."

"Ayna!" he called out loudly.

At once, a slender young woman appeared, with enormous expressive eyes and long black hair. She was fragile, and yet there was a strange emptiness in her gaze, as though someone had hollowed out her soul.

"Take our guest to her room," Saman said, without looking at her. "Is everything ready?"

"Yes, Master," the girl replied meekly, in a soft, almost whispered voice. She glanced at Maryam and motioned for her to follow.

They passed through the luxurious living room and entered a long corridor lined with identical doors on both sides. Maryam's room was at the very end. Ayna opened the door, inviting her inside.

A strange sensation washed over Maryam.

Déjà vu, she thought, and a faint smile touched her lips.

"What are you smiling about?" the girl asked.

"Oh, nothing," Maryam replied, looking around. "I was remembering how, not long ago, I was led to another room in much the same way. They called it the Blue Room."

"Why blue?"

"I don't know. That's just what those people called it."

"Were they also part of the Elite?"

"I don't think so. They were something else, but definitely not the Elite."

"Then why did you leave them?"

"I have to find my son," Maryam sighed.

The girl studied her carefully.

"And where is your son?"

"I don't know," Maryam answered, feeling the familiar lump rise in her throat again. "But they say he's being held where they keep teenagers... from thirteen to fifteen."

"That's not far from here," the girl whispered.

"What?!" Maryam gasped. "You know where they are?! Please, tell me!"

"No... I can't. I'll be punished. I've already stayed here too long." Her voice trembled. "I just... wanted to talk to an ordinary person."

"Please..." Maryam pleaded, looking into her eyes.

But the girl only shook her head.

"I can't... I'm sorry. The bathroom is there," she nodded toward a door. "You'll find everything you need in the wardrobe."

She left, quietly closing the door behind her.

Maryam was alone.

She had no strength left. She collapsed onto the bed, burying her face in the pillow, and burst into tears.

"Lord... how is my boy now?" she sobbed. "I beg You, Lord, please—help me."

At that moment, there was a soft knock at the door. Maryam wiped her tears and rose from the bed.

"Come in."

Saman entered and looked closely at the exhausted, tear-streaked woman, her eyes red from crying.

"Why are you crying?" he asked, as if the answer were not obvious.

"You know perfectly well why," she replied in a weary voice.

"But your tears will not help."

"And what will?" she asked quietly.

"You," he said. "You, Maryam. There is something in you that pleases the Creator greatly. That is why we need you."

"But why do you need me?"

"Renounce Him," he said softly, insinuatingly, stepping closer. "With us, you will receive far more... Power—and most importantly, your son. He will be treated like a prince. All the pleasures of the world will open themselves to you."

His voice flowed like honey, while his eyes remained cold.

He came closer, and Maryam felt sparks of pleasure rise from the tips of her toes upward. For a brief moment, they lingered in the lower part of her body, igniting a warm, pleasant fire, then surged higher. Her head began to spin, her thoughts clouded, and the world around her blurred...

She came to in her bed. Saman was sitting nearby in an armchair, his expression focused.

"You're awake, Maryam," he said in a velvety voice. "Excellent. Now take a shower, change for dinner, and don't be late. I don't like to wait."

He left her alone with her heavy thoughts.

Maryam rose and went to the shower. The cold streams brought her slightly back to her senses. She thought about how powerful his influence on her body had been—and how she was supposed to resist it. What was it? Hypnosis? A drug? Or something far more sinister?

Throwing on a robe, she knelt by the narrow window niche, folded her hands, closed her eyes, and whispered:

"Most High, hear me.

You are my only hope.

In You alone I see protection from my enemies.

I pronounce Your Name,

And my enemy trembles.

Do not abandon me.

Be my shield and my stronghold."

After the prayer, her heart grew calmer, and a quiet certainty settled within her.

She stood and opened the wardrobe. Inside hung an elegant black dress. What a pleasant fabric, she thought, slipping into it and putting on the shoes. She quickly gathered her hair and, without looking in the mirror, left the room.

The corridor greeted her with soft twilight, dispersed by an antique candelabra. Their dim light fell on paintings in heavy gilded frames, creating an atmosphere of mystery. Maryam walked along the thick carpet, barely hearing her own footsteps.

Before her appeared unusual doors—adorned with exquisite, almost magical stained glass, it shimmered in shades of amber, ruby-red, and sapphire-blue, flaring with every movement of light. Maryam stopped, mesmerized by the play of colors.

The stained glass seemed to breathe, to pulse, shaping strange outlines from chaos. Suddenly, figures emerged within the mosaic—indistinct, wavering, as if woven from moonlight. They bowed their heads in silent greeting and instantly dissolved, leaving only glimmers on the glass.

What kind of hallucination is this? Maryam thought, shaking her head to dispel the illusion. Am I dreaming? Or did they drug me again? I must be careful.

“Lord, save me,” she whispered barely audibly.

The moment she raised her hand to push the door, the doors opened silently by themselves, as if they had been waiting, inviting her inside.

A small man in black livery appeared before her. He bowed politely and gestured for her to follow.

They entered a spacious, brightly lit circular salon. The room breathed grandeur: comfortable emerald-velvet sofas lined the perimeter; in the center stood a massive round table, above which hung an enormous chandelier—an astonishing creation of metal and glass in the form of a falling angel holding seven candles. The sight was both mesmerizing and unsettling in its solemnity.

“Maryam, don’t stand there—come to the table,” Saman said with a satisfied smile.

The same majordomo escorted her to the table and seated her opposite the master of the house.

A violin began to play—a pure, piercing melody that made the heart ache. She searched for the musician and spotted him standing in the corner. Suddenly, new sounds joined the violin—a white grand piano by the window released enchanting chords. The fusion of instruments created something truly magical. Tears welled in her eyes. Everything felt unreal, like a scene from a fairy tale.

"Maryam, you are enchanting," Saman said in a voice that made her shiver.

Two young girls appeared and began serving exquisite culinary creations. Saman opened a bottle of red wine—Château Mouton Rothschild, 1990. Filling a glass, he handed it to Maryam with a smile.

"A magnificent bouquet."

Cautiously, she took the glass and inhaled the aroma, not daring to taste it.

"Drink, Maryam. It's not poisoned—you are far too valuable to us alive," he said in a hoarse voice.

Before sipping, she silently recited a brief prayer and took a small sip. The pleasant smile vanished from his face. It became serious—yet still attractive.

He poured himself wine, leaned back in his chair, and began:

"Maryam, we live here without need or suffering, unlike so many others. We are the Elite—the chosen. We have been granted power over people, over their feelings..." He smiled and leaned closer. "Over yours as well."

Maryam trembled again and mentally called out to Arizal. Instantly, Light filled her body, giving her strength to resist. She lifted her head and looked him straight in the eyes, imagining herself enclosed in a cocoon of Light. Gathering that energy, she directed it toward Saman.

He flinched, looked at her in bewilderment, stood up, and left the table, leaving her alone.

Maryam silently thanked her Teacher for the help, rejoicing in her small victory.

Less than five minutes passed before he returned.

"Maryam, you are truly magnificent," he said thoughtfully. "Your power of resistance is remarkable. I have never encountered anyone like you. I needed to understand how strong your resistance was—and you passed brilliantly. Most would have yielded long ago after experiencing the pleasure I offered." He studied her intently. "But you endured."

He fell silent, savoring the moment, as his cold, assessing gaze slid across her face, as if probing the deepest corners of her soul.

"I'm genuinely curious... how long will your resistance last?" He smiled enigmatically and chuckled softly. "I am proud of you."

Maryam remained silent. She had no intention of responding to this madness or playing his game.

She listened—but did not hear, focusing on maintaining her calm.

"Maryam," he said gently, almost tenderly, moving closer. "My dear Maryam... Together, we could create a new world. A world ruled by justice. A world without pain. A world where people are finally free..."

"First, give me back my son," she interrupted firmly.

"Yes, of course," his voice instantly turned cold and calculating. "But only after your consent."

"Consent to what?"

"You must renounce your Lord."

"You mean the Most High?" Maryam asked, raising an eyebrow. "Why?"

He burst out laughing—this time unpleasantly.

"Maryam, you are an intelligent woman. You must understand—one cannot serve two masters."

"Exactly," she replied with mild irony. "That's why I serve only one—the Most High. How could I serve another?"

"That is precisely why you must renounce Him and begin serving ours."

"And why should I renounce my Lord for yours?"

"Because your God constantly demands restraint and asceticism," he said. "He deprives you of joy and pleasure. With our master, everything will be different. You will enjoy life without limits, without prohibitions, without guilt."

He sighed, as if regretting her blindness, and continued, his voice growing softer, enveloping:

"Imagine it—no anxiety, no doubt, no fear of punishment. Only pure, boundless pleasure. You could have anything you desire: power, wealth, recognition. And your son—safe, honored, by your side. Isn't that what you want?"

He paused thoughtfully.

"But I suspect neither food nor pleasure will truly impress you," he said philosophically. "So, we offer you something greater: limitless knowledge, power, dominion over natural forces. We will teach you to control what others call miracles."

"So, you're offering me a deal," she said quietly. "My faith—in exchange for my son?"

"Not a deal," Saman corrected gently, tilting his head. "A choice. A choice between a world where you endlessly struggle for scraps of happiness, and a world where happiness is your natural state."

"Happiness without God is an illusion," she replied firmly, meeting his gaze. "You can promise me everything, but I know—without Him, even paradise becomes a desert."

Saman leaned back, crossing his arms. For a moment, irritation flashed in his eyes, but he quickly mastered himself.

"You speak this way because you've never truly lived," he said. "You exist in a cage of dogma and prohibitions. We offer you wings."

"The wings you offer are merely chains of another kind," Maryam answered. "They may feel light—but sooner or later, they will pull one down."

She lowered her voice, exhausted.

"Saman, show me my son."

"Very well," he replied calmly. "You will see him tomorrow afternoon from a distance. And he must not notice you. Otherwise, you will disrupt our entire system of education and undo the results of our hard work," he added with irony.

Maryam sprang from her chair as if struck by lightning and grabbed his hands.

"Truly?!" she almost cried out. "Are you telling me the truth?!"

Her voice trembled, tears ready to spill.

"Now, now, calm yourself," he said, watching her with strange admiration. "I am telling you the truth. What incredible strength you have..."

He summoned Ayna.

"Take Maryam to her room."

The girl nodded silently and headed for the exit. Maryam followed, still unable to calm herself. She tried to speak to Ayna, bombarding her with questions, but it was futile. The girl only looked at her sadly, sighed softly, and left without a word.

Maryam was alone again.

She slowly approached the bed, sat down on its edge, and closed her eyes for a moment. Everything that had happened that day crashed over her like a heavy wave: fear, hope, pain, exhaustion.

After reciting her evening prayer, she lay down. Sleep did not come easily; her thoughts circled endlessly. Again and again, Maryam whispered the words of prayer until, at last, she sank into a heavy, troubled oblivion...

And she saw that she was standing before an enormous bird, whose black wings wrapped around her, enclosing her completely. Such an overwhelming power emanated from the creature that the air itself seemed to thicken, turning heavy and viscous, like dense jelly.

Suddenly, Maryam tore herself free from its embrace and ran. She knew her chances of escape were almost nonexistent, yet her legs carried her forward on their own—toward a narrow recess where she could hide from this inexplicable, paralyzing fear.

But soon the bird appeared again, standing before her, emitting strange sounds, like the faint ringing of a bell. Everything inside her grew cold. Her body ceased to obey her will. Her mouth, against her will, tried to speak.

She clamped it shut with both hands, praying to God for help. But her body resisted, submitting to a чуждой—foreign—will. Again and again, she called upon God, begging Him not to allow her to utter the words the great bird commanded her to speak.

Suddenly, another bird appeared beside her, much smaller than the first. It spoke clearly and loudly:

"Invisible."

A dark mist enveloped Maryam, and now the enormous bird could no longer see her. The mist seemed to free her from the чуждой power, and she felt control over herself slowly returning.

CHAPTER 14
SHATTERED HOPE

The first glimmers of dawn barely broke through the dense clouds, staining the sky a sickly gray. Maryam opened her eyes and walked to the window. Beyond the glass stretched a bleak, desolate landscape that no longer brought her any joy. Once, she had loved greeting the morning, admiring the blue sky, the pale clouds, and the vivid green of the leaves. Now those simple pleasures felt like distant memories, fragments of a life that no longer existed.

Lord... will it really be like this forever? she thought, turning away from the window and heading to the bathroom, grateful for the simple comfort of running water.

After completing her morning rituals — changing into clean clothes and offering her prayers — she sat down in a chair, her gaze fixed on the door. Time seemed to stretch endlessly. Every minute felt unbearably long. Unable to endure the oppressive stillness any longer, she finally stepped outside.

The overcast sky pressed down heavily, low and suffocating. Not a single soul was in sight. Grim, silent buildings surrounded her, resembling abandoned sets from a disaster film. She moved forward cautiously, glancing around with unease, half-expecting something monstrous to leap out from behind a corner and attack her.

Ahead, several buildings were arranged in a tight circle around a massive central structure. Behind it rose a tall fence topped with barbed wire, concealing a long building that resembled an industrial hangar. Nearby stretched a field with an arena — a sight that pierced her painfully, reminding her of the one she had once seen at Dimyon's place.

So they hold their bloody games with infected people here as well, Maryam thought bitterly, quickening her pace toward the hangar.

Suddenly, voices echoed nearby. Several people stepped out onto the road. Panic surged through her. She pressed herself against the wall, holding her breath, silently praying that she would not be noticed.

Phew... I think I got away with it.

And then—

The world before her eyes blurred. A powerful wave of weakness washed over her, heavy and crushing. A sharp ringing filled her ears. Her head spun, and her body went limp, flooded with a strange, unnatural warmth. An overwhelming urge to sleep overtook her.

Through the haze of semi-consciousness, she whispered the words of a prayer. Gradually, the ringing subsided, and her mind cleared, though the weakness still lingered.

Gathering the last of her strength, Maryam rose and, on trembling legs, made her way toward the hangar.

There it was — the fence topped with barbed wire. She circled it carefully until she noticed a small, nearly invisible door.

Locked.

How am I supposed to get inside? she wondered. Even if she somehow managed to climb the fence — which seemed nearly impossible with that vicious wire — the area was far too exposed. She would be spotted immediately.

Closing her eyes, Maryam reached out in her thoughts, trying to connect with Arizal.

And — oh, joy — it worked.

In an instant, her body filled with light, and glowing symbols appeared above the door — the very symbols her teacher had once taught her. She read them aloud. The coded lock responded and clicked open softly.

Maryam gently closed the door behind her and hurried toward the hangar.

I hope no one noticed me, she thought as she slipped inside.

Before her stretched a vast rectangular hall, individual rooms lined the perimeter, while a training area occupied the center of the space. The artificial lighting was dim, barely illuminating the interior. Somewhere in the distance, the steady hum of a generator echoed through the structure.

Her heart pounding, Maryam crept along the rows, peering through the windows.

Inside each room sat teenagers — her son's age. They were immersed in various activities: some reading books, others studying languages, a few locked in intense chess matches, while several played Monopoly with quiet but genuine enthusiasm.

She passed nearly all the rooms, but her son was nowhere to be seen.

Tears filled her eyes as she reached the last room — and froze.

He was there.

Beside him sat Saman, reading aloud from a book, while the boy turned a Rubik's Cube in his hands, his brow furrowed in concentration.

A burning desire to rush forward and embrace her son overwhelmed her completely. She took a step—

And in that very moment, strong hands seized her from behind. A rough palm clamped over her mouth, cutting off her breath, and she was dragged away.

Startled, she froze for a heartbeat, then bit down hard on the hand covering her face. The man cried out and cursed, but did not loosen his grip. On the contrary, he tightened it, leaving her no chance to resist.

Dragging the struggling Maryam into a room, he threw her to the floor. The door slammed shut behind them, and over his shoulder, he snapped:

"Don't do anything stupid."

CHAPTER 15
THE RESCUE

Exhausted and broken by grief, the woman sat in the middle of the room and sobbed.

All the pain of her aching maternal heart was tearing its way out.

Her son—her precious child—had been so close. She had only needed to stretch out her arms to embrace him, to hear his voice, to look into those beloved eyes...

Again and again, the same image rose before her: her boy, alive and well, sitting beside Saman.

Pain gave way to indignation.

No. I will not surrender. I have to do something...

"Lord, please help me," she whispered.

A frontal assault was useless.

She would have to act according to a different principle:

By submitting, you overcome.

Very well. She would play the role of obedience. She had nothing left to lose.

The most important thing was that her son was alive and appeared healthy. With the rest—God willing—she would cope.

Having convinced herself of this and calmed down slightly, she sank into prayer, remembering her son, Khalid's family, her teachers, and even... Saman.

Forgive him, O God, for he knows not what he does...

A knock sounded at the door. Maryam flinched.

Saman entered, unleashing a stream of reproaches:

"Maryam, what are you doing? You are like those unfortunate Adam and Eve, who could not wait for their destined hour and tasted the apple too soon. Why the haste? Did I not promise that you would see your son after noon? What is the point of such impatience?"

She raised her eyes to meet his gaze.

"Saman," Maryam whispered submissively, lowering her head, "a mother's heart knows no peace when her child is in danger."

She looked at him, then lowered her eyes again and spoke even more softly:

"To know that your son is nearby and yet be unable to see him—that is beyond my strength. Please forgive my lack of restraint. I could not act otherwise."

Saman studied her in silence, as though weighing her words. Then, unexpectedly, he smiled.

"Well then," he said calmly, "you are a woman, and impatience is natural to your kind. I understand. But you must learn to control such impulses. It is important."

He paused, then added:

"And now, I suggest we take a short walk."

He gallantly took her arm, and familiar warm sparks ran through her body.

I must admit, it feels pleasant, she thought, allowing herself for a brief moment to surrender to the sensation...

Then she jolted inwardly.

No. Stop. I will not allow myself to be drawn into this game again.

Maryam silently recited a prayer, and the spell retreated, allowing her to focus on her surroundings.

The path led toward a central building that rose majestically above all the others.

"Look, Maryam," Saman said almost reverently. "From this building, our Leader governs the world. You are being offered a unique opportunity—to join us and become part of our world. Together with your son, you could become his assistants."

"Believe me," he continued, "such an offer is a great honor. One single word—yes—and all earthly blessings will open before you."

Maryam allowed herself the faintest smile.

Oh, of course. As if I would believe you. The moment I say "yes," your brotherhood would descend upon me, and I would become a slave to your so-called Leader. No. You will never have my soul—not for all the treasures of the world. Better a terrible end than endless nightmares.

"Saman," she asked calmly, "this Leader of yours... who is he?"

"In the world of men, there are presidents," he began enthusiastically. "Our Leader is also a kind of president—but not of one country. Of the entire world!"

"Understand, Maryam," he continued, growing more animated, "a new world order is coming—one man ruling the world, and we, his helpers. Just imagine such power!"

Yes, I can imagine, she thought. And I also know that in the end, you will have to pay the price.

"Saman," she said aloud, "could you give me a tour inside the building?"

"Of course!" he exclaimed eagerly. "Soon, that will be possible for you. One word—yes—and all doors will open before you!"

For some reason, the film Jumanji flashed through her mind—the same seductive fervor, the same honeyed persuasion.

"Welcome to Jumanji," she almost laughed, but quickly caught herself.

Saman looked at her in surprise.

Maryam took his hand and hastily continued:

"It sounds tempting..." she said aloud.

Inside, she decided: You must know your enemy by sight in order to understand who you are dealing with.

Suddenly, noise erupted—shouts, cries, sounds of violence.

"What is that?" Maryam asked anxiously.

"I have no idea," he frowned, trying to steer her aside—but he was too late.

People emerged onto the road, dragging captives whose appearance evoked pity. They stumbled forward under the rough shoves of guards.

Two figures caught Maryam's attention—a man and a woman, their hands tightly bound, their clothes torn, faces smeared with dirt and bruises.

"What is happening here?" she repeated in horror.

"These are the ones who disobeyed our master and refused to serve him," Saman replied coldly. "Look closely. This is the fate of those who reject our terms."

"What terms?" Maryam asked, her voice trembling.

"Do not worry," he said smoothly. "This does not concern you. You are a clever woman. You will not create conflict. Isn't that right, my dear?"

The words "my dear" sent a shiver through her.

I have to help them somehow, she thought feverishly.

"Tell me, Saman—where are they taking them?"

"To a place from which they are unlikely to return," he replied darkly.

"And if—while I consider your proposal—nothing is done to these people?" Maryam asked, looking him straight in the eyes.

He studied her with interest.

"Bravo, Maryam! Your self-sacrifice is exquisite how you humans love to sacrifice yourselves! To offer up your own soul in order to save people you do not even know—how magnificent!"

"And what exactly do you expect me to do with them?" she asked.

"Are the rooms next to mine occupied?"

He frowned.

"No."

"Then they should be housed there."

"No."

"Why not?"

"Because my house is not meant for such scum."

"But my soul is not cheap either," she said firmly.

He paused, thinking.

"Very well. There is a small shed beneath your window. I will have it cleaned. They will be placed there."

"Thank you, Saman. And please—do not forget to feed them."

"As if I wouldn't have thought of that without you," he snapped irritably. "Enough surprises for today."

"We are going home now."

"And my son?" she pressed. "You promised I would see my son."

"You have already seen him. That is enough. You are asking too much."

"No, Saman. This is not too much. For now, it is a necessity."

"A necessity?" he echoed.

"For a mother to see her son. You would not understand."

He took her by the hand and escorted her to her room.

“Put yourself in order. Thanks to you, I have not had a single bite all day. I am hungry as a lion.”

“So am I,” Maryam admitted with a faint smile.

When he left, she closed the door and sat on the edge of the bed, sinking into the thoughts of the day. Her nerves were stretched to the limit.

She undressed and stepped into the shower. Warm water flowed over her body, gradually washing away the accumulated fatigue.

“Lord,” she whispered, “only let me have enough strength.”

After drying herself with a soft towel and slipping into a robe, she knelt down. Again and again, Maryam asked the Almighty for wisdom and strength for the trials ahead.

When she finished praying, she rose, straightened her shoulders, and forced herself to smile.

Never despair, and always carry the Light within you, she recalled her teacher’s words. Only then can you change the world around you.

In the wardrobe awaited a black skirt, a white silk blouse, and high-heeled shoes.

“I agree to everything,” she muttered, “but why such high heels?”

When she was ready, she let her long hair fall freely and approached the mirror. A woman with burning eyes and a faint blush on her refined face looked back at her.

Despite all this suffering... I still look rather attractive, she thought with mild irony.

Leaving the room, Maryam headed toward the unusual stained-glass doors.

"How strange," she noted. "The patterns keep changing."

The glass shimmered with living colors, creating the illusion of movement. The doors glided open, inviting her inside.

The salon greeted her with renewed splendor. Tonight, the table was draped in a black cloth embroidered with gold. Above it hovered a magnificent chandelier—an angel figure darkened with gold patina, radiating a mysterious crimson light. Classical music, played by unseen musicians, filled the room with an air of mystical ceremony.

"My dear Maryam, I am delighted that my efforts to please your refined aesthetic taste have met with approval," Saman declared with the gravity of a count.

So much pathos, she thought, watching him. An actor—nothing more.

The same thin majordomo in a black livery approached and politely helped her take her seat opposite Saman.

"Tonight, Maryam," he announced, raising a crystal glass, "I propose a toast—to your future with us. A small celebration."

"And what exactly are we celebrating?" she asked, masking her anxiety.

"Our Leader is ready to meet you," he proclaimed solemnly, as if delivering a royal decree.

The blood drained from her face. The ground seemed to give way beneath her feet.

"So soon? I'm not ready..."

"Do not worry. I understand your excitement perfectly. To meet the Leader himself—such an honor is not granted to everyone."

God forbid such an honor, she prayed inwardly.

"Tomorrow, at three in the afternoon, you will be presented to the Head of the Elite in the main hall," he continued.

Her face turned pale as linen. Her temples throbbed.

"What will I be expected to do there?" she whispered, desperately seeking a way to postpone this "great meeting."

"Do not be afraid, Maryam. Tomorrow you will simply be introduced—nothing more. It is merely an acquaintance."

"Yes..." she managed, a lump rising in her throat.

"Why are you so nervous?" Saman whispered, stepping close. "Little coward."

He took her hands, and she heard her own heart pounding.

"Maryam, everything is fine... calm down," he murmured, his voice soft, almost lulling.

Gently stroking her head, he pulled her toward him and kissed her.

Energy surged like a powerful wave, flooding her consciousness and spilling through her entire body. Overwhelmed, she staggered and collapsed.

What was that? she thought when she awoke in her room.

Lord... how could I allow his poison to penetrate my body? No. Absolutely not. One must never yield to this force. The moment you think, "I'll try, I can handle it,—you are already hooked.

Her lips trembled with a bitter smile.

This time, I lost, she admitted to herself. One must never even allow the thought: "I am stronger than this." Such thoughts must be cut off at the root. The severing of sinful thoughts is the only way to battle passions.

Passion does not arise in the human soul at once. Everything begins with a thought. A thought is born from sensation, from impressions, from what is seen, or as an image imposed by the enemy. It comes without a person's consent or participation. But one is given the right to choose: to accept the thought into the heart or to reject it.

The struggle is not to eliminate thoughts altogether, but to refuse them the power to govern our actions—to acknowledge their existence without allowing them to weaken the soul by taking root and decaying within.

Maryam sighed.

Yes... Thoughts not cut off in time are like weeds in a fruit garden. They spread—and soon the roots are poisoned, the fruit ruined. And the result is always the same: defeat.

She sank to her knees, and words poured forth from the deepest place within her:

"Lord, help me in the battle with my thoughts.

I beseech You, O God, deliver me from the seduction of the vile enemy and shelter me from his snares.

Grant me, O Most High, strength and steadfastness to withstand his temptation, to remember Your holy Name and not renounce You out of fear of the enemy."

Maryam rose and walked to the window. Below, in a small house, a warm light flickered softly. She remembered the people she had saved that day. Opening the window, she whistled quietly—an art her husband had once taught her.

"He whistled like the Nightingale Robber," they used to laugh back then.

"Oh... those were the days. May the Almighty help him," she whispered.

Maryam whistled again. A man appeared at the window below. He looked up suspiciously at first, then, as if remembering something, smiled.

"I'm coming to you," she called softly, climbing out of the window.

Thank God it wasn't high, but when she landed, she couldn't help letting out a quiet groan—her leg was still aching, ever since she had fled from Dimyon and jumped unsuccessfully from a tree. Rubbing the sore spot, Maryam quickly slipped into the little house.

A woman standing by the table gasped softly in surprise. She froze for a moment, peering at Maryam—then recognition dawned, and she smiled. She looked to be no more than fifty: thin, with simple, kind features and attentive, slightly weary eyes.

"Hello," she said. "My name is Sarah." "Hello. I'm Maryam."

"And I am Dimitri," the man added. "Dimitri... how interesting. You wouldn't happen to be a clergyman, would you?" Maryam asked.

"Yes, exactly so—you guessed right."

"How did you end up here?" Maryam asked. Dimitri sighed heavily.

"I was married, and we had two children—a son, five years old, and a daughter of twelve. One day, my wife went to visit a friend, and Sarah, the children, and I stayed home. And then... then came the explosion... Lord, have mercy. I know nothing about my wife. We escaped, were picked up by a vehicle, and brought here. At first, they treated us very well —fed us, entertained the children, created the illusion of care. And then they began to pressure us to renounce God. Of course, we refused. After that, they took our children." His voice trembled, but he quickly steadied himself.

"We don't know what has happened to them. They tortured us like the Forty Martyrs of Sebaste," Dimitri added quietly. "First with cold—where they even got so much ice at this time of year, I have no idea. They put us into barrels filled with ice and kept us there. When they saw we still would not renounce God, they threatened us with a furnace. They said we were certainly no Three Holy Youths who survived the fire—and that we would serve as firewood."

"And... did they put you into the furnace?" Maryam asked.

"No, they didn't go that far," Sarah replied with a bitter smile. "You intervened in their plans for harvesting 'environmentally friendly firewood' for tonight's dinner."

"Well... I'm very glad I did," Maryam said quietly. "Otherwise, what would I have told your wife, Dimitri?"

"My wife? What do you mean?" he asked in surprise.

"Your wife's name is Alexandra, isn't it?" "Yes—Alexandra... I used to call her Sanya. But how do you know her?"

"I met her beyond the Wall."

"She's beyond the Wall?" Dimitri's eyes lit up. "How glad I am for her! Glory be to God!" "Tell us—how is it there?" he asked eagerly. Maryam briefly told them about her time with Arizal.

They listened, holding their breath.

"What a blessing that Alexandra is there with them," Dimitri said softly. "If only we knew where the children are. And how did you end up here, Maryam? And why did they listen to you—and let us go?"

Maryam told them of her ordeals.

"Yes..." Dimitri murmured. "How precious your soul must be to them. What a heavy cross you carry. But God does not give trials beyond our strength—if He has given it, then you will endure."

"Tomorrow, they plan to present me to their Leader," Maryam said quietly. "I am afraid, but I must go. I have to save my son. And then we will find your children and try to escape from here. But... how?"

"Maryam," Dimitri said gently, "let us entrust ourselves to God's will. Let us pray. Morning is wiser than evening."

"And what is that story about the Forty Martyrs of Sebaste?" Maryam asked.

Dimitri began to speak.

In the year 313, Emperor Constantine the Great signed a decree granting freedom of religious worship. His co-ruler, Emperor Licinius, signed the same decree for the territories under his authority.

Around the year 320, a Roman legion was stationed in the city of Sebaste, in Armenia. Among those soldiers were forty deeply devout warriors, natives of Cappadocia. Their commander, Agricolaus, demanded that they offer sacrifice to pagan idols—but the soldiers refused.

They were arrested, bound, and led to a frozen lake near the city. It was winter, and the evening was falling. The warriors were stripped naked and placed into the ice-covered water. A brutal cold seized the bodies of the holy martyrs, and they began to freeze.

Their torment was especially cruel because, on the shore of the lake, a warm bathhouse had been prepared as temptation. Anyone who wished to save his life only had to declare to the guard that he renounced God—then he would be allowed to enter the bathhouse and warm himself.

All night long, the warriors endured the merciless frost with courage, encouraging one another and singing sacred hymns to God.

At dawn, one of the soldiers could no longer bear the suffering. He left the lake and rushed toward the bathhouse. But the moment warm air touched his body, he collapsed and died. Soon after, the prison guard, Aglaius, saw an unearthly light shining above the martyrs who remained in the lake. He was so shaken that he, too, came to believe in God. He tore off his clothes and joined the thirty-nine martyrs. When the torturers arrived later, they saw that the warriors had not frozen at all—indeed, they seemed warmed. Enraged, the executioners shattered their legs with hammers, threw them into fire, and afterwards cast the charred bones of the martyrs into the river."

"That was an enlightening and moving story, Dimitri," Maryam said quietly.

"And what about the story of the Three Youths?"

Dimitri continued.

“The king of Babylon, Nebuchadnezzar, was an idol worshiper. He ordered the construction of a massive golden idol and commanded that everyone bow down before it at the sound of the trumpet.

Anyone who refused would be thrown into a blazing furnace.

So when the trumpets sounded, all the people fell to the ground. Nebuchadnezzar rejoiced in his greatness. But soon his servants reported that three young Jews—Hananiah, Mishael, and Azariah, friends of Daniel, who had studied alongside him—remained standing and did not move.

‘These men,’ the flattering informers said, ‘do not obey your command, O king. They do not serve your gods, nor worship the golden image you have set up—though you intended to place them over the affairs of Babylon.’

The king flew into a rage. ‘Why do you not obey my command?’ he demanded. ‘I will throw you into the furnace—will your God save you from my hand?’

They answered him calmly: ‘Our God, whom we serve, is able to deliver us from the burning furnace and from your hand, O king. But even if He does not, know this—we will not serve your gods or worship the golden idol you have set up.’

Nebuchadnezzar was overcome with fury; his face was distorted with rage. He ordered the furnace heated seven times hotter than usual and commanded his soldiers to bind Hananiah, Mishael, and Azariah and throw them into the flames.

The fire was so intense that the soldiers who carried out the command were killed by the heat. But the three young men fell into the furnace bound, and the fire did not touch them.

They stood and walked amid the flames, singing praises and blessing the Lord. Azariah prayed and glorified God's Name. Seeing this, the servants added even more fuel, but the Angel of the Lord descended into the furnace and drove the fire away, creating a rushing, cool wind in its midst. The flames did them no harm at all."

"That is the story, dear Maryam," Dimitri finished softly.

"Thank you," she said, rising. "I must go." Dimitri walked her to the window; his eyes filled with sincere concern.

"Maryam, please let me help you climb back."

"No, Dimitri, thank you. I'm not going back to my room just yet. I need to walk and gather my thoughts."

"I'm afraid it's dangerous," he said gently. "May I accompany you?"

"No. Stay with Sarah—your help is needed here," she replied firmly.

"Maryam, are you sure? I cannot let you go alone," he said anxiously.

"I'm sure. You are needed here. Pray."

She headed toward the hangar.

The night was silent, the air taut with tension. Standing before the door entwined with barbed wire, she closed her eyes.

"Teacher..." she whispered.

Familiar letters flared softly above the entrance. Maryam spoke them aloud. The door opened, and she slipped inside.

Moving quietly along the wall, she reached the last cell.

Here... this is where I saw my son last.

Her heart pounding wildly, she reached for the handle—

"Oh no... no..." she gasped.

Samon stood before her.

"Maryam," his voice was gentle, almost tender. "Did you truly think you could deceive me?"

He stepped closer. The lamplight caught only part of his face—his eyes glowed with a strange, almost inhuman light.

"My dear, I am always near you—even when you do not see me. My energy is inside you. I feel you. I hear you. There is nowhere you can hide from me. Do you hear me?" he whispered against her ear, pressing her to the wall.

"No," she snapped inwardly. "That won't work on me again."

Without hesitation, she struck him hard in the groin. He doubled over in pain, and Maryam burst into the room.

Her son was not there.

"Where is my son?!" she screamed. "Where is he? Do you hear me? Answer me! Please!" "Maryam," Samon said coldly, straightening. "Enough hysteria. Your sentimentality means nothing to me. I may know what you feel—but you will not see your son until you complete the rite."

"What rite?" she whispered, barely moving her lips.

"The rite of initiation to Him," he pointed downward,

"and renunciation of Him," he lifted his finger upward.

"At least tell me where he is."

"He—like all the others in his group—is undergoing the process of renouncing God." Maryam shuddered.

"It is not easy for him," Samon continued, a faint smile touching his lips, "but there has been progress. And when we finally claim him completely—it will be a truly precious prize." Samon stepped closer and looked straight into her eyes—coldly, piercingly, as though he were scanning every thought in her mind. His fingers closed firmly around Maryam's elbow. With a light yet inexorable motion, he led her out of the room and down the corridor, all the way to her chamber.

The door slammed shut with a dull, hollow sound.

Pausing on the threshold, he turned back and said quietly:

"Maryam... you are making foolish choices again. Our patience is not without limits."

The door closed.

Thousands of thoughts swirled through her mind. She exhaled sharply.

Stop.

She needed to pray. She needed to calm herself.

She focused on her breathing.

Inhale... exhale...

And when her heart finally eased its frantic pounding, she spoke:

"Lord, now more than ever I need You.

You are my shield and my support;

In You alone I place my trust.

I ask You, Lord—help me.

Not my will, but only Yours be done.

Not as I say, but as You decree.

Here I stand before You,

and I surrender myself completely into Your hands.

Deliver me from evil.

Do not let me perish.

Save people, and all children,

from the darkness that rules the world today." She lay down, and sleep came quietly, wrapping her in a soft veil of visions.

She dreamed that she was a tiny bud growing on a great Tree—the Tree of Man.

He had lived much and learned much.

He had studied under learned men,

had sought knowledge tirelessly, and had delved into the mysteries of existence. Once, he experienced a great fall.

Crushed and deeply disillusioned,

he went in search of truth and met a wise man, who taught him great and ancient wisdom. Then he saw the Light.

He reached for it and drew it into himself, filling the vessel of his soul to the brim.

Only then did he understand what it meant to receive happiness—

and realized that happiness could be shared. From that moment, he saw the world differently.

He felt great.

He became like a vast tree, spreading wide branches.

Some branches he nourished with sap—they grew upon him, stretching toward the Light alongside him,

afraid to break the fragile spell of enchantment.

Others he allowed to grow only so that, having drunk their fill of sap,

they might taste what it meant to be happy. And once he had filled them with his own energy and the energy of the sun, he used them merely as reserves—

drawn upon whenever his own mighty strength ran low.

He no longer cared for those branches. What more could he take from them? Even their leaves had already been taken. But one branch proved strong.

It refused to remain dependent on the Tree.

It possessed the strength to become a tree itself —for it had been shown the sun.

Once, that branch had been a tiny bud.

In its dreams, it had seen what happiness truly was—

a happiness far greater than what the Tree had ever shown it.

In dreams, that happiness granted it freedom. In dreams, it flew, touching silver dew— sensations it would never forget.

It remembered how angels came to it,

took it by the hands,

set it gently in place,

and stepped back.

When it lifted its gaze,

it saw the Light above—

a Light it would never forget.

A torrent opened above it—

no, not a torrent,

but a downpour of silver—

and it filled the branch completely.

And that was happiness.

No...

Bliss.

No—there were no words in this world to describe it.

Only angels could bestow such a gift.

The Tree could only imitate it.

For angels need nothing from us.

They rejoice simply in watching us bloom, grow, and become covered in silvery light. They nourish us with their love and joy. But the Tree, in its grandeur and intellect, had learned much,

had understood much.

It spread its roots deep—

they needed nourishment.

It thought greatly,

dreamed of becoming even greater.

But its ego interfered.

It grew greedy.

It gave sap to its branches less and less. And the branches began to wither, to die. Yet the Tree did not understand that only the one who gives much receives in return— a hundredfold.

One cannot only take.

For in a single moment, one may lose all strength and become nothing more than an empty vessel.

So reasoned the little branch.

Having fallen, it tried to take root in the earth —but it lacked the strength.

Lying on the ground, it gathered all it had left and remembered what its dreams had taught it that it must grow on its own.

That it must reach for the Light.

It prayed.

It called upon the angels.

And it dreamed again.

In that dream, it was drowning.

It sank to the bottom—

but after a moment, it understood:

the strength was still there.

It surged upward.

Oh God—how difficult it was.

The first level was passed.

Then the second.

And then—the third.

The most difficult of all.

It nearly gave up.

The water grew dense and heavy,

pressing against its chest like a crushing ring. The branch gathered all its strength and rushed upward.

Just a little more— the Light was already visible.

The level that had seemed the hardest of all.

It passed it.

Dawn had barely touched the sky when Maryam opened her eyes.

The dream still lingered at the edge of her consciousness—blurred, yet insistent: a small branch breaking through the heavy water toward the Light. She blinked, dispelling the vision. This was no time for reverie.

Quickly washing and offering a short prayer, she slipped soundlessly out through the window. Carefully passing the small house where her new friends slept, she moved in the opposite direction from the hangar.

Keeping to the shadows of the buildings, Maryam crept toward one of them. She slipped inside and hid behind a recessed niche in the wall, pausing to assess her surroundings.

The room resembled the place where her son and the other adolescents had been kept. Along the far wall stood narrow, tiered bunk beds, where children slept.

Suddenly, a lock clicked.

The door burst open with a loud crash, and several people entered the room. They switched on a harsh, glaring light and began roughly waking the children.

The younger ones started to cry. The older ones rose silently and obeyed without protest.

Their task was simple: to dress quickly and wash.

Any hesitation was met with a brutal lesson. Those who hesitated were punished by those who were ready sooner than the others.

The offenders were forced to their knees, and their peers were ordered to deliver sharp slaps to their faces, each blow accompanied by shouted insults. Those who refused to strike were punished themselves.

This vicious cycle turned children into little monsters, cultivating cruelty, cowardice, and betrayal.

"Lord, save these children," she cried out in a burning prayer.

At that very instant, a blinding flash flooded the room, forcing the overseers to scatter in terror.

Mariam sprang from her hiding place and rushed toward the children. Frightened, they recoiled from her.

"Children... don't be afraid. I will help you. Not all of you yet—I can't manage that alone. Right now, I need only two of you: Darya, twelve years old, and Ilya, five. Your father is Dmitry. Where are you? Come to me." Silence followed.

Dozens of wary eyes stared at her. Someone sobbed quietly.

"Children, this matters," she said. "I promised your father I would bring you. Then I will come back for the rest of you."

"We're here," said a girl with two braids, stepping out from behind the corner, holding a small boy by the hand.

Mariam rushed to them and pulled them into a tight embrace.

"Thank God. Let's go."

But they had barely taken a few steps when cries erupted from all sides.

"Take me too!"

"Me too!"

Children reached for her, clutching at her clothes. Mariam struggled to hold back her tears. Keeping her voice steady, she spoke calmly but firmly:

"Listen carefully. You must all calm down now and behave as if nothing happened. No one must know I was here. Do you understand?" She scanned their faces.

"Otherwise, the overseers will return, and things will become much worse. I will come back for all of you. I promise."

She grabbed the children's hands and rushed toward the exit.

They were almost at the door when pounding footsteps and heart-rending crying erupted behind them.

She turned and saw a little boy, three or four years old, his face streaked with tears, running after them with outstretched arms.

"Take me with you! Please, take me!"

"Oh Lord... what am I to do?" she whispered —and without hesitation scooped the child into her arms.

Now the three of them—stumbling, gasping— ran toward the exit.

The saving door was just ahead. An ancient Name escaped Mariam's lips, and they slipped through inside.

"Thank You, God," she breathed, seeing the familiar little house.

At that moment, Ilya tripped over a stone and fell, bursting into tears.

Without thinking, Darya lifted her brother into her arms. Together they rushed inside, nearly colliding with Dmitry and Sara, who stood by the stove, calmly preparing something from the food Saman had allotted to them.

Seeing Mariam with the children, they froze like statues, unable to speak, unable to believe their eyes.

Mariam had to walk over to Dmitry and literally place the sobbing Ilya into his arms. Only then did the shock break. They came alive, embracing and soothing the children, laughing and crying at once.

Only the youngest child stood apart, hugging himself and sobbing softly.

“What’s wrong, little one? Come here,” Sara said gently, stepping toward him and pulling him into her arms.

“What’s your name?”

“Andrei,” the boy whispered, burying his face in her dress.

“My God... Mariam, how did you do this?” Dmitry exclaimed, finally finding his voice.

“Father Dmitry, not now. Questions later,” Mariam said urgently.

“Pack quickly and leave. Behind the house, there’s a path to the main entrance. Run to the gates—there will be a guard shift change. I watched them: at that moment, they wandered off to chat and exchange news. This is your chance.”

She spoke quickly, precisely.

“Take all the food—it will be useful, not just for you. When you cross the field, be careful. If you see people, throw the food and run.”

She explained in detail how to reach Khalid’s family—and then the Great Wall.

“And what about you?” they asked anxiously. “I’ll be calmer knowing you’re gone. Otherwise, I’ll worry about you, too.

It hurts that I couldn’t tear my son from their claws... but with God’s help, I will find a way.”

They prayed together.

Dmitry helped Mariam climb back through the window, and they left.

“God, help them,” Mariam whispered, watching their figures disappear into the darkness.

Her heart tore itself apart between joy for the ones she had saved and the pain for her son still trapped in the hands of those monsters.

CHAPTER 16
MEETING THE HEAD

A GLIMPSE OF HER SON

As far as she could, she followed them with her eyes.

There is nothing more I can do for them, she thought.

With a heavy sigh, she undressed quickly, slipped beneath the blanket, and pretended to be asleep.

The door burst open without a knock.

Saman stormed into the room. His eyes hurled lightning.

“Maryam!” he roared.

The woman, feigning drowsiness, slowly emerged from beneath the covers and stared at him in confusion.

“How—how are you here?” he thundered, his voice shaking with rage.

“Where else would I be?” she asked sleepily. “Did something happen?”

“Stop pretending!”

“I don’t understand you, Saman. You burst into my room without knocking, you shout, and you explain nothing. Please—explain,” she said, sitting on the bed, hugging her knees, the picture of innocence.

He exhaled sharply, barely holding back a scream.

"Your friends," he said through clenched teeth, "the ones you 'helped'... escaped. And they took three children with them."

Maryam barely managed to suppress a sigh of relief. They made it.

But she forced her face to remain blank.

"And yet," he continued, narrowing his eyes, "I fail to understand how they managed it. They do not possess such power. That kind of power exists only in you. Or are you lying to me?"

One step—and he was beside the bed.

Instinctively, Maryam burrowed deeper under the blanket, as if she could vanish into its folds. But Saman would not allow it. He grabbed her by the legs and yanked her off the bed.

"Listen to me carefully," he hissed, setting her on her feet like a rag doll.

His steel gaze drilled into her eyes, as though trying to turn her soul inside out. He seized her chin and forced her to look at him.

"Do not dare lie to me."

Maryam swallowed convulsively. Her breath faltered; her heart pounded so violently she was certain it could be heard beyond the walls.

He pulled her closer. Her thoughts began to blur. A warm, enveloping wave spread through her body, dulling her will, softening her resolve. The urge to surrender was almost overwhelming.

But one thought hammered relentlessly in her mind:

Enemy. Beware.

She shook her head sharply and called upon God.

One single word—“Save”—shattered the spell.

Maryam tore herself from his grip.

Saman cursed under his breath. His eyes narrowed in fury—but something else flickered there as well: not quite anger, not quite admiration.

“I never cease to marvel at your strength,” he said with a crooked smile devoid of warmth.

“Get dressed. The reception will begin soon.”

He turned and left, slamming the door behind him.

On trembling legs, Maryam made her way to the bathroom and splashed cold water on her face.

“Lord, this is so difficult... help me,” she whispered.

The mirror reflected a pale stranger, eyes burning with feverish intensity.

Back in the room, she dropped to her knees and prayed for a long time. When her heart and mind finally grew still, she focused inward and tried to reach Arizal.

At first—nothing.

Then, slowly, her awareness began to rise... higher and higher, toward a source of Light. Up there, everything was calm, peaceful—so peaceful she did not want to return.

Suddenly, a familiar voice sounded:

— Maryam.

— Yes, Teacher,— she replied, holding her breath.

— Remember what I taught you: there is no time and no space—everything is illusion.

Freedom from death comes only through knowing the Truth.

Truth belongs to the inner realm; the path to it belongs to the outer one.

Only by walking this path will you know Truth—and become free from death.

Be strong. Walk without fear. Darkness comes and goes, driven back by Light.

Everything in this world casts a shadow—darkness is merely Light's reflection.

Do not be afraid. This is your destiny.

Remember the Name of the Most High that I taught you."

His presence faded, and another voice followed—firm, steady:

"Maryam, the darkness we pass through leads us to the Light.

In the Name of the Lord, you will overcome him.

Do not fear—we will not abandon you."

For a moment, there was silence.

Then came a third voice—warm, achingly familiar:

— Maryam, my daughter,— Khalid said gently.

Remember: only love can defeat darkness.

Bless it, no matter how painful it is.

Do not allow hatred into your heart. Pray.

And if Satan incites you—seek refuge in the Most High, for He is All-Hearing, All-Knowing." (7:200)

"And now—return."

Maryam slowly opened her eyes.

Her entire body burned with heat—it felt as though one more moment and the room itself might ignite from her presence. She took a deep breath, closed her eyes, and visualized her energy condensing into a sphere, which she carefully placed within her heart.

"That will be safer," she chuckled softly to herself.

"Otherwise, they might not even let me step outside this house.

I probably look like a ball of lightning right now."

A soft knock sounded at the door.

Aina entered the room without a word and placed a breakfast tray on the table.

So, today I'm dining alone, Maryam thought with a faint, ironic smile.

Perfect. At least it's quieter here. I wonder what delicacies they've prepared for me this time.

She examined the tray: toast with jam and a pleasantly fragrant drink.

"Hm..." she murmured to herself. I think I'll stick to my little rusks from "Seraphim of Sarov." Somehow, they feel... safer.

She poured the drink out the window and tossed the toast onto the roof, where crows were always circling. Strangely enough, after the explosion, these birds had proven remarkably resilient—unlike most other creatures—and continued to inhabit the area.

Soon there was another knock, and Saman entered the room.

"Have you eaten?" he asked, casting a satisfied glance at the empty plate.

"Excellent."

"Thank you very much," she replied gently. "Everything was delicious—especially that unusual drink. By the way, what was it made of?"

"That is not important," he said curtly. "Here. Put this on."

"For what purpose?" Maryam asked, taking the bundle. "What's wrong with the clothes I'm wearing now?"

"They do not meet the requirements of the upcoming ceremony," he answered coldly.

Ceremony? Maryam tensed.

"But you said that today I would only be introduced to your Head."

"That is true," he replied, "but you must be dressed according to protocol. You wouldn't go to church in shorts, would you? The same principle applies here. There is a dress code."

"But this isn't a church."

"That depends on how you look at it."

Maryam took the bundle and went into the bathroom. As she changed, she couldn't help noticing the symbolism of the outfit.

Black—the color of mystery and power.

Red—the color of blood and life.

She slowly slipped into the black dress, then draped the cloak with its hood over her shoulders. The inside shimmered with crimson silk.

"Well, look at that," she muttered, studying her reflection.

"Straight out of a movie about secret orders."

She turned away from the mirror, sat down, and exhaled deeply. When her thoughts finally settled, she lifted her heart toward the Most High in a fervent prayer.

O Most High, my enemies have multiplied,

and many rise up against me.

Many say to my soul: "There is no salvation for you in God."

But You, O Lord, are a shield around me.

I cry out to You and I know that You hear me.

You will not give me a trial beyond my strength.

I am afraid, yet I do not fear my enemies who surround me on every side, for I believe that Your shield is before me.

Lord, I am a great coward—and I wonder whether this trial is truly within my strength.

I beg You: do not abandon me.

She rose, straightened her back, and stepped outside.

Saman was pacing the room impatiently. When he saw her, he snapped irritably:

"Maryam, as a true woman, you may allow yourself to keep a man waiting—but not me."

He studied her closely, then gave an approving nod.

"Excellent. You look as you should. Let's go."

"At least they gave me comfortable shoes," Maryam muttered under her breath as she followed him.

They approached the central building where, according to Saman, their Head resided. The closer they drew, the tighter her heart clenched with anxiety. Suddenly, she felt the ground slip away beneath her feet, and a crushing weakness washed over her.

Lord... no... not now, she managed to think—before consciousness left her.

Darkness.

How peaceful it is in this silence.

But light—persistent, probing—began to tease her eyelids, forcing her to awaken. Slowly returning to herself, she opened her eyes. The surroundings were strange, unfamiliar.

Trying to understand whether this was a dream, Maryam sat up and realized she was in a vast circular hall designed in an Art Deco style. A majestic ceiling loomed above, adorned with a grand chandelier shaped like a descending angel. In its hands were seven candles, and three more crowned its head.

She recalled that Saman had a similar chandelier—but that one lacked the three candles on the head. This one, however, was staggering in scale.

At the very center of the hall, like a point drawn by a compass, stood a throne with a high back, crowned at the top. Enormous dragon claws served as its legs, and lion heads formed the armrests, lending it a terrifying aspect.

Around the perimeter, in nine concentric rows, stood other seats. In one of them, in a place of honor, sat Maryam herself.

What happened to me? she tried to recall.

I didn't eat or drink anything... Well, just a few sips of water. Bastards.

Fine. Let's see what you're planning.

Her body had gone numb from the awkward position. She tried to stand—but her legs would not respond, as if paralyzed.

So, they've added paralysis to the program, she thought grimly.

All right. Don't panic.

Though the thought frightened her, she whispered:

"Lord, have mercy..."

Suddenly, she felt the numbness recede. Her legs were free again.

Whew. Thank God. And they won't know a thing.

At that moment, a heavy door creaked open, and Zar entered.

His usually cold, impassive face was now twisted into a mocking grin.

Traitorous face, flashed across her mind like subtitles on a screen.

He glanced in her direction and, wearing a cynical smile, walked forward. A moment later, Saman entered behind him. They both took their places on either side of the central throne-like chair. Soon, eight more men filed into the hall and seated themselves in a wide circle.

A wave of unease washed over Maryam. She lowered her head, closed her eyes, and began to pray silently.

Suddenly, someone touched her shoulder.

She flinched and opened her eyes.

Before her stood a tall young man, no more than thirty-five. Chestnut curls fell softly across his forehead, and his dark, deep, almond-shaped eyes held a strange fusion of wisdom and cruelty. A quiet but tangible power emanated from him, as if the very space around him responded to his presence.

Who is this? flashed through her mind.

"Good evening, Maryam," she heard a low, pleasant voice—steady, confident, commanding.

"Good evening," she replied, striving to conceal her unease. "Who are you?"

"I am the one who will save this world."

Of course, she thought with biting irony. No more, no less.

He smiled gently, as though he had read her sarcasm.

"You don't believe me?" he said softly. "You should."

An icy chill spread through her chest. Try not believing him, she thought. Such power radiates from him... Could this be their Leader?

"Yes, Maryam," he said calmly, "you are correct. I am exactly who you just thought of."

She shuddered almost imperceptibly.

"So... you can read minds?"

"Not entirely," he replied with a faint smile. "But almost. I see the thoughts of many. Yours—only in part. You are extraordinary... and that makes you particularly interesting."

"And what exactly makes me so interesting to you?"

"First of all," he answered, "because you are not like the others."

"Oh yes," she smirked, casting a sideways glance at Saman. "I hear that a lot."

"Maryam," he said quietly, almost with sympathy, "what troubles you so deeply?"

She lifted her head and looked straight at him.

"You know perfectly well. Why did you take my son?"

"Your son is better off here. He will be raised as a true warrior."

"A warrior of what kind?" she asked sharply. "A warrior without a soul?"

"My dear," he said indulgently, "what is a soul compared to power and all the blessings of this world? I will give him everything—strength, honor, pleasure. He will live a long, happy life."

"By selling his soul to you?"

"The soul, the soul..." he drawled with mild mockery. "You all speak of it as though anyone has ever seen it. Tell me—what makes it so valuable?"

Maryam closed her eyes for a brief moment, then quietly recited:

"Then the Lord God formed man of the dust of the ground, and breathed into his nostrils the breath of life; and man became a living soul."

She raised her gaze.

"Genesis, chapter two, verse seven."

The Leader froze—then burst out laughing.

"Maryam, you are astonishing!"

"Yes," she replied evenly, glancing once more at Saman. "I've already heard that today."

He stepped closer. His voice softened—but grew more dangerous.

"Do you truly believe all these... fairy tales?" His eyes narrowed. "Tell me—where exactly in those words do you see proof of a soul? Where is the evidence of its existence? And what, precisely, is its worth?"

"Forgive me," she interrupted calmly, changing direction to steady herself. "But you still haven't introduced yourself."

He tilted his head slightly and smiled with one corner of his mouth.

"I will introduce myself in time. For now, everyone calls me the Leader. You may do the same. After all, a name matters far less than the purpose with which we come into this world."

He raised his hand, as though drawing an invisible line in the air.

"My purpose is to save the world. Look around—see how much suffering there is. And who caused it? People. And who governs people? God. Your God, who watches all of this and allows it to happen. Can you not see how cruel and indifferent He is?"

"No," she replied firmly. "I do not see that. God did not create this—people did. God created us to be happy. He gave us everything we needed for that. But blinded by our egoism, we allowed evil to rule us. By living this way, we cut ourselves off from the ability to perceive the Creator. That is why we became cold and afraid. A void formed within us—the absence of Light—and we began desperately searching for something to fill it."

She paused, meeting the Leader's gaze directly.

"But we search in the wrong places. People try to fill themselves with smartphones, games, alcohol, drugs, and shopping—things that delight for an hour and then leave emptiness behind. These are temporary pleasures, and their joy is fleeting. It is like a scale with a neutral line in the middle: the higher pleasure rises above it, the further it plunges below. A +1 is always followed by a 1—often far worse than what came before the stimulus. And that suits the dark system perfectly."

She glanced at the Leader.

"They eagerly offer people new 'toys'—anything to keep them asleep. While a person is entertained, they grow blind. Blind and unable to behold the face of the Almighty. Humanity was created in the image and likeness of God. What does likeness mean? It means that in the Creator, there is no desire to receive—only the desire to give. God created humanity to fill us with Light—with all blessings. But humanity sinned and fell. Fell into a world of egoism, where immense inner work is required: to transform egoism into altruism, to become like the Creator."

She spoke steadily, with quiet conviction.

"And when that happens, a human being becomes a living reflection of Him. Our perception of the world is shaped by our desires. When those desires are corrected, a person perceives the Creator. The Higher Light is always in perfect stillness and never changes. It does not alter its nature of giving. All changes in our lives come from changes within us. Improve your inner world—and the quality of life improves with it."

— Our dear Maryam, — the Head smirked, — you seem remarkably well-informed.

He tilted his head, studying her with feigned curiosity.

— But if we follow your theory, then all the chaos in the world exists because the inner world of humanity never changed.

— Does that mean the Creator made imperfect creations? — he laughed.

— No. The Creator made us perfect. But the sin of Adam and Eve gave us work to do upon ourselves. On the other hand, without that fall, there would have been no work at all. They would have lived in a perfect world, basking in the Creator's Light — and none of us would exist.

She paused, gathering her thoughts.

— Adam knew Eve only after the Fall. Before that, they did not know physical desire. Which means that all of this was part of the Creator's Design from the beginning. "Nothing moves below unless it is decreed above."

They had to fall into an imperfect world, to labor upon themselves, to earn the Creator's Light rather than receive it freely — without the Bread of Shame, the pain of receiving a gift without effort.

The Head cut her off with an irritated exhale.

— Fairy tales. All of it — fairy tales written by your sages.

Show me this corrected world. Show it to me!

His voice thundered beneath the vaulted ceiling.

— Look around you! Look at what humanity has become!

You destroyed the earth. You dried the rivers, burned the forests, poisoned the air you breathe. You cut off the very branch you were sitting on.

— Not without your help, — Maryam replied quietly, but firmly.

— Man is born free and has the right to choose his master, — he said philosophically.

The Head stepped closer, testing her gaze.

— And most of you gladly choose our master. It's easier. It's simpler to walk a smooth road than to climb a mountain.

But... — he smiled thinly, — at the end of the road, the price must be paid.

— Maryam, these discussions are beneath you. You deserve more. I will give you power — power over people and over the forces of nature themselves.

— Watch, — he breathed, raising his hands.

In that instant, the air trembled. His body arched, his eyes shut — and suddenly an ear-splitting crack of thunder tore through the sky. The hall seemed to shudder from within.

A violent storm erupted: lightning split the heavens, thunder shook the earth, rain poured down in a solid wall, and the wind howled like a wounded beast. The elements raged without restraint.

Maryam clutched the back of her chair, barely able to remain standing.

Then, just as suddenly, the Head lowered his arms and exhaled deeply.

Silence.

The storm vanished. Sunlight broke through, and the world sparkled with raindrops.

— You see, Maryam, — he said, his eyes burning with wild fire, his hair disheveled, making him both terrifying and strangely beautiful. — This is what I can teach you.

— Come, — he said. — Let us go outside.

They stepped beyond the building. The sun blazed on the wet stone tiles.

He whistled.

Crows descended.

He spoke a short, guttural phrase — something like a croak. The birds listened attentively, then answered and flew away.

— What did you say to them? — Maryam asked, unable to hide her astonishment.

He turned toward her, smiling smugly.

— I ordered them to bring me a rabbit sitting beneath the old tree at the edge of the grounds.

Before she could even process the words, the crows returned — a rabbit clutched in their claws. They landed before the Head and gently laid the animal at his feet.

He picked it up, stroked it — and tore off its head.

Maryam didn't even have time to gasp. She stood frozen, staring in horror.

Then he stroked the rabbit again, pressed the head back into place — and before her eyes, the flesh knit itself together.

The rabbit revived.

He set it on the ground, and it scampered away.

— You see, — he whispered, locking eyes with her. — I can grant life.

And I can teach you how.

His voice was soft, almost hypnotic.

Maryam felt something tighten inside her — not fear, but the terrifying awareness that this was power.

— Now, — he said calmly, — let us return.

They re-entered the building and passed through the grand hall into a long corridor lit by torches. The Head opened the door to a small, intimate sitting room.

Soft furniture. Muted light. The scent of age and quiet.

— Sit down.

Maryam obeyed, lowering herself into the chair.

For a moment, he simply watched her. Then he said:

— Show me your leg.

— Why? — she asked, startled.

— Not long ago, you injured it while fleeing from my people, — he smiled. — It still troubles you. Allow me to make amends for their roughness.

Surprised, Maryam extended her leg.

The instant his fingers touched her skin, an overwhelming wave of bliss flooded her entire body. For a brief moment, she lost herself completely, surrendering to the sensation.

Then — within her inner vision — her Teacher appeared.

He looked at her with deep care, his vast eyes filled with concern. His lips silently formed the Name of God.

Maryam shook her head and spoke that Name aloud.

Everything vanished — the pleasure, the paralysis.

She opened her eyes.

The Head was watching her with open admiration.

— Yes, — he said quietly. — You are strong. Saman did not exaggerate.

But I had to be certain myself.

He rose and stepped closer.

— Well then… we shall work together.

— With whom? — She asked warily.

— With you, Maryam, — he smiled. — I have never made such an offer to anyone before. But to you — I do.

You are needed. I offer you partnership. Together, we will rule the world.

He leaned closer, his voice softening to a whisper.

— Come now… say yes.

Maryam lifted her gaze.

— Before anything else, Head, tell me where my son is.

Show him to me.

— Very well. You will see him now.

— You will really show him to me right now?

— Yes. Come.

They returned to the great hall. He beckoned Zar and whispered something into his ear. Zar bowed and hurried away.

Maryam stood there, unable to remain still. She shifted from foot to foot, wrung her fingers, and prayed silently. Every second stretched into eternity as she waited for this meeting.

At last, the doors swung open.

Zar entered — and behind him stood her son.

Maryam could not hold herself back. She rushed toward him, seized him, and pressed him tightly against her. Startled, the boy froze, afraid even to move. Unable to believe his eyes, he whispered:

— Mama... Mommy... is it really you? Mama, say something. Let me hear your voice — then I'll believe it.

Her poor heart felt as though it would burst. A lump rose in her throat, stealing her words. She covered his head and face with kisses, lifted him like a little child onto her lap, rocked him, stroked his hair.

— My son... my precious boy... how long I searched for you, — she whispered.

— That's enough of these displays, — a cold voice sounded behind her.

— Your wish has been fulfilled. You have seen your son. Time is up.

Maryam raised her head. Her eyes shone with tears.

— How can this be... what are you doing? We've only just met... Please, I beg you, give us a little more time.

— No, Maryam, — he answered firmly.

— But if you agree to our terms, you will be together. Always.

He stepped closer.

— You will have a home. You will live there and help me rule the world.

Merciful God... Tears streamed down her face.

Lord, I beg You, help me... please help me, she whispered soundlessly.

— Enough, — he growled.

— Zar, take the boy away.

— No! — she cried out. — Please...

Zar stepped forward and seized the boy by the hand.

— Mama... Mommy... don't cry. Don't cry, Mommy, I'm strong. I'll manage! — the boy shouted, though tears poured down his own face.

They took him away.

Once again, he was torn from her.

Maryam collapsed into the chair, utterly drained. There was no strength left for anything. Inside, there was only emptiness — corrosive, devouring her entire being.

— Saman! — he called.

— Take Maryam to her room. She needs time to think... and to make the right decision.

He looked at her searchingly.

— Isn't that right, Maryam?

Silence answered him. Not a word. Not a movement.

Saman approached, bowed respectfully to the Head, then carefully took Maryam by the hand. She did not resist. Obediently, like a shadow, she rose and followed him, seeing nothing around her.

He led her to her room, left her there, and departed.

Maryam sank to the floor. She wrapped her arms around her knees and sat rocking gently, staring at a single point.

This happens when pain becomes unbearable.

No strength. No emotion. Only a ringing emptiness inside.

A person seems to fall into an abyss where there is nothing at all.

It is the soul's protective response to overwhelming pain.

From a psychological perspective, inner emptiness can be described as a profound loss — a state in which something essential has left one's life, while something new and sustaining has not yet arrived. A person feels hollow, sorrowful, and drained of energy. Interest in one's own life fades; joy and pleasure become difficult to find. Apathy, indifference, depression — these become constant companions.

But she could not allow herself to drown in that emptiness.

She had a son. And he needed her.

What do they want from me? Why me? What is so special about me? What good can I bring to this world? They need me for a reason — not by chance. That means much depends on me.

Perhaps I have no right to think only of my son. I must think more broadly. Didn't the Head say, "I will save the world"? Then I must save the world from him.

But how?

She lifted her face toward the sky and whispered:

Lord, if only You would open Your plan to me — just a little... if only You would show me what You require of me. At least give me a sign.

Gathering the last of her strength, she rose, dressed, and stepped out into the courtyard. The damp air struck her face, clearing her thoughts ever so slightly.

CHAPTER 17
THE DRAGON

THE BEGINNING OF THE PROPHECY

Deep night had settled outside.

A cold wind tugged at her hair as she wandered through the deserted streets, weighed down by heavy thoughts.

Why do they need me? What is my true role in all of this?

These questions tormented her soul, echoing like Shakespeare's eternal dilemma: to be or not to be.

Without noticing, Maryam found herself on the outskirts of the compound.

Suddenly, an unfamiliar roar pierced the silence, a sound unlike anything she had ever heard in her life.

Her blood ran cold. Every instinct screamed for her to flee as far away as possible.

But curiosity, as always, won.

She moved toward the sound.

Before her stood a massive structure, smoke billowing from within, the terrible roar rolling out of it like thunder. Holding her breath, Maryam pushed open the heavy doors and froze in horror.

Standing before her was a real dragon.

Enormous. Crimson-red.

A heavy chain hung from its massive neck.

It had seven heads and ten horns, and upon each head rested a diadem.

Its vast, ancient eyes, filled with centuries of dark wisdom, were fixed upon her.

Its entire body was covered in golden scales, and its tail, ending in a star-shaped tip, swayed slowly from side to side.

At that very moment, stars suddenly appeared in the night sky, and, as if obeying its will, began to move in rhythm with the dragon's tail.

Maryam shook her head, trying to understand whether this was a dream.

Then a voice thundered directly inside her mind:

"So... you have come."

This was the beginning of the prophecy.

She recoiled in terror, unable to comprehend how the creature had entered her thoughts.

"Do not be afraid," the voice responded within her.

"For now, I cannot harm you. You are needed."

"I've been told that more than once," she replied quietly, without lifting her eyes.

"But I would very much like to understand — why am I needed? And for what purpose?"

Slowly, one of the dragon's heads rose, and once again its deep, resonant voice filled her being:

"Your soul is high and pure, and the mission you carry within you is great."

"I see," Maryam frowned slightly.

"But why do you need me?"

"Take up your cross and renounce this world. In doing so, you will save it."

Her brow furrowed.

"What does that mean, take up my cross?"

"You are destined to make a great sacrifice. Only then can the world continue to exist."

She lifted her gaze.

"And you? Why do you need this?"

The dragon sighed heavily. All seven of its heads bowed toward her.

"According to prophecy, when the final day comes, He will cast us into Tartarus, and we shall burn there forever. No one desires such a fate."

It fell silent for a moment, then continued more softly, almost sorrowfully:

**"Once, I was a great angel. I beheld the true Light.

Now I am condemned to remain here on earth, feeding on human darkness instead of rejoicing in the songs of my brethren.

I was the first among equals.

They called me the Morning Star."**

He looked at her with his immense eyes — and there was no malice in them. Only infinite weariness.

**"And who am I now? An executioner? A warden for convicts who do everything to please me?

I am tired...

Yet humanity continues to sin endlessly. But the day will come when He descends to cleanse your world, and then we will be forced to depart forever, with no salvation for us."**

His gaze sharpened.

"But you... You can change everything."

"Me?" she whispered.

"What can I possibly do?"

"You have a great mission. You can save us.

Renounce Him — for our salvation."

The words pierced her heart.

What a choice...

Lord, is this truly what awaits me?

Will I endure it? What do you want from me?

I must save the world from him... But who am I?

He says, "I will save the world if I renounce You; then I will perish, but the world will continue to exist."

But what kind of world would that be, a world ruled by him?

No. I cannot allow this.

“Most High,” she prayed silently, “nothing exists outside Your control. I give myself fully into Your hands and will never renounce You, under any circumstances.”

The fragile woman stood like a statue beneath the night sky, hands folded in prayer, her gaze lifted heavenward.

The dragon watched her with interest, not interfering, and then, like thunder from a clear sky, his voice burst into her thoughts:

“Maryam, you will have to sacrifice yourself.

You are a mother, and mothers are inherently weak.

You will not endure your son’s suffering.”

She flinched and looked up sharply.

“What do you mean?” she asked tensely.

“That you will yet witness,” he replied coldly.

“Like a lamb, he will be led to slaughter.

And you are far from Abraham’s holiness.”

She closed her eyes and turned inward to God:

“Let God arise, and let His enemies be scattered;

let those who hate Him flee from before His face.”

The dragon recoiled violently.

His pupils narrowed, and he staggered back as if struck by an invisible force.

When he spoke again, his voice no longer echoed in her mind:

"You are strong, mortal, but only for a time," he growled, having lost his ability to read her thoughts.

Good, she thought. He can no longer hear me.

If Abraham was willing to sacrifice Isaac, and God prevented the bloodshed, then I, too, will not be abandoned.

But Abraham was asked to act on his own, and God stopped him.

What will I do if they begin to torture my son? I will not endure that.

Lord, help me. If You have placed me here, then I must be able to endure. Grant me a burden according to my strength.

She glanced at the dragon with pity.

I feel sorry for him, she thought.

Once he beheld You and was nourished by Your divine Light... How far he has fallen.

The dragon twitched his tail nervously, staring at her, trying again and again to pierce her mind, but the light surrounding her left him no way to approach.

At last, his patience snapped.

"Why are you standing there in silence?" irritation slipped into his voice.

Maryam raised her eyes.

“Nothing. It’s late, and I’m very tired.

May I go to sleep?”

“Go.”

She left.

Her head throbbed, her body burned with fever, and her legs barely held her. She reached her room with great effort, but did not make it to the bed.

She collapsed onto the floor.

When consciousness finally returned to her, she could not understand where she was, whether it was day or night.

Aina was sitting beside her.

“Maryam, you’re awake! Thank God. We were so worried about you.”

“What do you mean, worried?” Maryam asked weakly. “Was I asleep for a long time?”

“Yes... You were unconscious for more than two days,” Aina replied gently, her eyes full of concern.

Startled, Maryam tried to sit up, but the room spun. She fell back onto the pillows.

“Don’t get up,” Aina said softly, adjusting the blanket. “Lie still for a while. You can try later.”

“Aina... tell me honestly... did I really sleep for two whole days?”

"Yes," she nodded. "When I came into your room, you were lying on the floor, unconscious. I tried to wake you, but nothing worked. Saman came too. He sat beside you for a long time... but you showed no signs of life. We were... frightened for you."

"I don't think Saman was frightened," Maryam said quietly, then added warmly, "but thank you, Aina. Truly. For caring."

She embraced her.

Aina froze for a moment, surprised, then hesitantly returned the hug, deeply moved.

"I'm sorry, Maryam," she said shyly. "We're not supposed to... show simple human feelings. But I can't get used to that."

"And why should you?" Maryam asked softly. "Tell me about yourself. How did you end up here?"

Aina lowered her eyes, as if gathering courage, then began to speak quietly.

"I was still a teenager when Zar found me. My parents died early, during the epidemic. I survived as best I could. Only faith in God kept me from losing my mind."

She smiled sadly at the memory.

"Then Zar appeared. So handsome, confident, imposing. He began to take care of me. At the time, I thought fate itself had sent him. And I fell in love... He suggested I move in with him. And then... everything changed."

Her voice grew heavier.

"He forbade me to pray. Said it was nonsense, an invention for the weak. At first, I resisted. It was very hard. I cried, argued... but then I got used to it."

She sighed, staring into the distance.

"Every day, he repeated that God doesn't exist, that humans evolved from apes, and that man governs himself. Over time, I began to agree. His ideas stopped hurting my ears."

Aina smiled bitterly.

"A beautiful life, comfort, pleasure, abundance, did its work. Faith in God stopped being important to me. And then the explosion happened. Everything collapsed. He brought me here. Now I rarely see him, but every day they check whether I've started believing again in that 'ridiculous idea' that God exists and created us."

Tears welled up in her eyes.

"But honestly, Maryam... deep down, I believe God exists. That He is the Creator of the universe, the Architect of this world, and that everything is connected. The way He designed everything down to the smallest detail... It's incredible."

She paused, lost in thought.

"Once, I read a book about how the DNA of wheat and human DNA are remarkably similar in structure. Can you imagine that? Human DNA and wheat DNA — so alike. And yet wheat's DNA is far more complex — about seventeen billion base pairs."

Maryam listened in awe.

"That's five times larger than the human genome," Aina continued thoughtfully.

She wasn't merely speaking — she was reflecting aloud, marveling at the mystery of life itself.

"The main difference between humans and wheat," Aina said softly, "is that wheat cannot influence the quality of its growth. It has no free will. But humans do. We have this extraordinary ability — to shape the growth of our bodies, minds, and consciousness. We can choose our path because we are free."

She smiled sadly.

"But unfortunately... people often choose what harms their body, soul, and spirit."

Maryam listened without interrupting. When Aina finished, she stepped closer and embraced her gently.

"Aina... you are incredibly wise. How did you manage to survive here, among all of this?"

"If you want to live, you learn how to adapt," Aina replied with a humorless laugh.

Then she hesitated.

"You know, Maryam... when I was little, my grandmother and I used to sit by the fireplace in the evenings. She would knit and read holy books aloud. Those were good times."

Her voice trembled with nostalgia.

"Wheat was often mentioned in those books."

For a moment, Aina fell silent, as if returning to the scent of smoke, the warm lamplight, the hands of her grandmother, smelling of wool and bread.

"There is a very interesting parable," she finally said.

"The Parable of the Sower."

She closed her eyes, as if once again hearing her grandmother's voice...

The Kingdom of Heaven is like a man who sowed good seed in his field.

But while people slept, his enemy came and sowed weeds among the wheat and went away.

When the plants sprouted and bore grain, the weeds also appeared.

So, the servants of the master of the house came and said to him,

'Master, did you not sow good seed in your field? How then does it have weeds?'

He said to them, 'An enemy has done this.'

The servants said to him, 'Then do you want us to go and gather them?'

But he said, 'No, lest in gathering the weeds you uproot the wheat along with them.

Let both grow together until the harvest, and at harvest time I will tell the reapers:

Gather the weeds first and bind them in bundles to be burned, but gather the wheat into my barn.'"

(Matthew 13:24–30)

Aina opened her eyes and looked at Maryam.

“What do you think this means, Maryam?” she asked quietly.

“I’ve reflected on this parable many times, but every time I arrive at a different conclusion...”

Maryam smiled, her eyes soft and luminous.

“I think,” she said gently, “that this speaks primarily about the cunning of unclean forces about how falsehood is mixed into truth, disguised as something that resembles truth, so that people may be deceived more easily.

“The Sower is our Lord,” Maryam continued.

“He sowed the seed of truth within human hearts. That truth fell into their souls and, in some, it sprouted. But even here there are difficulties: the seed may grow, yet the unclean force scatters its own seeds, doubt, clever reasoning, distorted wisdom, and a person, believing they have understood the truth, ends up in a dead end.”

She paused and smiled.

“There’s an old saying: ‘Where things are simple, there are a hundred angels; where things are overcomplicated, there are none.’

Faith must be simple, like a child’s. Only then is it alive.”

Aina listened without blinking.

“And the servants of the house?” she asked. “Who are they, in your view?”

“The servants...” Maryam repeated thoughtfully.

"I believe they are those who serve God, regardless of denomination. Their task is to help the seed grow within the human soul and to nurture a true shoot of truth."

"And the weeds?" Aina whispered.

"The weeds are people who have failed to live rightly. The hour will come when they are gathered into bundles and burned. But those who are wheat, those who bear good fruit, will remain and serve the Light."

She spoke softly, yet with quiet certainty.

"You see, Aina," Maryam continued gently,

"At first glance, this parable contains the entire essence and meaning of human life, which is likened to wheat.

"A person passes through stages of growth much like wheat does. Only the 'seed' of a human is not the body, but the spirit, the spirit that shapes all forms.

"Wheat is a seed, and for it to bear fruit and continue its life, it must first die and decompose in the soil. Only then does new life begin within it. A sprout appears, and it must break through the earth, overcoming resistance, striving upward toward the sun. It is labor. It is pain. But without it, there is no growth."

She smiled quietly.

"And so, it is with a human being.

We, too, are born from a seed, tiny and seemingly insignificant, yet carrying immense information about the future person. From that seed, a human is formed. They grow, they develop... and then they must turn inward, die to their former life, and be born into a new one, passing through the pain of birth.

“Pain purifies. Suffering transforms us.

The seed dies so the sprout may live.

The soul suffers so that the spirit may awaken.”

Aina listened, holding her breath.

“Maryam,” she said almost in a whisper, “how I wish I could spend more time with you... But you need to eat, and I must go. Otherwise...”

She hesitated.

“I will be punished.”

At that moment, there was a knock at the door. Without waiting for an answer, Saman entered.

“Good afternoon, Maryam,” he said with exaggerated courtesy.

“I’m very glad you’ve finally come to. We were worried. Your recovery took far too long.”

Then he smirked.

“Resistance,” he added. “The soul fights.”

His gaze fell on the untouched tray of food, and his expression darkened.

“Aina, what is this? Why has our guest still not eaten? The food must be cold by now.”

Aina paled, but before she could speak, Maryam intervened.

“Oh, Saman,” she said quickly, protecting the girl,

“I was just about to eat. Please don’t worry. Everything is fine.”

She forced a tight smile. She had no appetite, but under Saman's piercing gaze, she whispered a brief prayer and made herself swallow a few bites of vegetables.

"These prayers of yours..." he muttered. "They make me sick."

He stepped closer and ran his hand over her hair. Familiar, invigorating sparks coursed through her body. For a brief moment, it felt good, and she caught herself wishing he wouldn't remove his hand.

Saman seemed to read her thoughts. He smiled slyly and left, closing the door behind him.

Maryam exhaled deeply, shaking off the weakness, and stood up. Her head still felt slightly light, but overall, she felt steadier.

"I must pray," she whispered and sank to her knees.

The words did not come at once. She closed her eyes and breathed deeply. Her pulse slowly calmed, her heart settling into a steady rhythm.

"O Most High, guide me through this new day.

Grant me inner harmony, so that I may meet all that awaits me with dignity.

Teach me to accept Your will without condition and to trust it with my whole heart.

Be my guide in every moment of this day, support me through trials, and lead me along the true path.

Reveal to me Your purpose for my life and grant me the wisdom to understand it."*

CHAPTER 18
REFLECTIONS ON GOOD AND EVIL

THE CONFESSION OF THE FALLEN

After the prayer, her mind cleared, and the anxious thoughts receded. Maryam put herself in order and left the room. She walked quietly down the corridor, listening to every rustle. Somewhere nearby, muffled voices could be heard.

Suddenly, the doors to the sitting room swung open, and the tall figure of Zar appeared before her. His face, as always, bore an expression of cold calculation.

“Where are you heading, Maryam?” he asked.

“I’d like to look around,” she replied calmly, careful not to reveal her unease. “I can’t stay locked in my room all the time.”

Zar smirked but said nothing. He merely gestured with his hand, letting her pass.

Maryam entered the sitting room. Several people were seated at a massive table, speaking quietly among themselves. Her heart skipped a beat when she noticed Saman among them. He rose, his familiar, almost deliberately pleasant smile appearing on his face.

“Maryam! How are you feeling?”

“Much better, thank you,” she answered restrainedly.

"I just decided to take a short walk."

Saman studied her attentively.

"Very well. But remember—we have much to do, and your presence will be required soon. Don't go too far."

"All right," she muttered and stepped outside.

Cold wind struck her face. Maryam inhaled deeply, letting the frosty air clear her thoughts.

All right... I need to think this through. Too much has happened all at once: the explosion, my son, Arizal, Saman, the Head... the Dragon.

The Dragon...

What binds me to him? I feel it, some invisible thread connects us. But what could unite us? I stand on the side of Light, and he stands on the opposite side. Light and Darkness. Upper and lower realms.

She recalled Dante Alighieri's Divine Comedy. To escape Hell, the characters must turn themselves upside down at the point of greatest gravity, the loins of the Devil, and cross into the Southern Hemisphere. Virgil instructs Dante to cling to his neck as they descend the shaggy body of Lucifer. At the hip, Virgil turns upside down, continuing the movement, and when they emerge onto the rock, Dante is astonished to see Lucifer left behind—upside down.

Back then, it had reminded her of childbirth: to be born into the light, a child must also turn headfirst, pass through the mother's womb, and emerge into the world. A kind of death for the former life, and birth into a new one.

What is the analogy here?

Perhaps this is where the deeper meaning lies: just as Dante's soul passed through an experience of death in the depths of the earth to be reborn into new understanding, so too must a human being pass through the metaphorical death of the old self to be born anew, on a higher spiritual level.

The same is true of wheat: to bear fruit, it must die and decompose, and only then does the seed give rise to a new shoot that reaches toward the sun.

What does this lead to?

If one imagines a cross, there is a vertical axis—above and below—intersected by a horizontal line. When the lower rises (when a human being grows spiritually, ascending from below upward), and the upper descends (when Divine Light flows from above downward), a remarkable union of opposites occurs at the center.

At that moment, the vertical line rotates ninety degrees, and everything comes into balance: above and below find themselves on the same plane. They unite and reach equilibrium.

Perhaps this is how the world will come into balance—when above and below align, correction occurs, and opposites are reconciled.

But what is the power of the middle?

Balance?

Does evil transform?

What is the relationship between good and evil?

Is the power in faith? In knowledge? In change? In transformation?

Is this the Tree of the Knowledge of Good and Evil?

And perhaps the vertical line is the Tree of Life.

If so, what is my role in this vast equation of being?

“Ugh... God, help me understand,” she murmured, rubbing her temples. “This mystery still lies ahead of me.”

She sighed and gazed at the gray sky.

The Dragon spoke of sacrifice. Perhaps they need me to sacrifice myself for him... Most likely, the sacrifice must be voluntary, an offering made with forgiveness in mind.

But how can it be voluntary if my son is a hostage?

She fell silent, staring into the clouds.

And yet... if all of this is true, perhaps the long-awaited balance between good and evil will finally come. Evil will nullify itself and be forgiven. The world will return to its original form due to this world and be reborn, like a child.

Maryam laughed softly, tiredly, bitterly.

But why me, O God? What a task you have set before me. How can I manage all of this, stay alive, save my son, and rescue all the other children? I promised them...

Without noticing it, she had wandered to the edge of the settlement.

Before her stretched a bleak landscape: an endless gray field, here and there patches of new growth, and isolated leafless trees standing like charred posts. The sight was desolate.

And then, very close by, a low voice spoke, the Dragon’s voice:

“Thinking about the fate of the world?”

Maryam flinched and turned sharply. Before her stood a tall, imposing man with piercing dark eyes filled with millennia of sorrow.

“Who are you?” she asked, instinctively stepping back.

“You know,” he replied calmly.

“I don’t want riddles,” she said, turning away as if to leave.

“Listen, Maryam,” he said more gently. “You were born for this sacrifice. You are the only human who pitied me and who prayed to the Creator for me. I am grateful to you for that.”

“There’s nothing to thank me for,” she replied quietly. “I truly pity you. You were once the greatest of all angels... What drove you to betrayal? How could you turn against the Creator? Why? In your angelic nature, there was no place for envy, pride, or lust for power. How did these feelings awaken in you?”

The Dragon stepped closer. Darkness seemed to thicken around them; the air grew dense and heavy. His eyes, deep as the abyss of ages, locked onto hers.

“You ask the right questions, Maryam,” he said softly. “But the answers are not as simple as you think. When the Light became too bright for me, I began to see its flaws. Perfection felt suffocating. Order felt like a prison.”

“But isn’t that the essence of existence?” she asked quietly. “Order, harmony, love...”

“Love?” the Dragon scoffed. “What if love is an illusion? What if behind the mask of Light there is the same Darkness, just wrapped differently?”

Maryam shook her head.

"No. I can't believe that. Light and Darkness are not the same. They are opposites—like good and evil."

"And what if I told you that good and evil are illusions as well?" His voice grew quieter, more penetrating. "What if all of this is merely part of a single whole? I was created before the concepts of 'good' and 'evil' existed. Before humanity. Before sin entered the world.

"Yes, I envied. I loved the Creator and wanted to be special to Him. But when He discussed creation with the others, I was not allowed to attend the council. I was denied knowledge of His plans. That disturbed me deeply. I believed myself to be His favorite."

He spoke bitterly.

"I wanted to be as great as God Himself, but I could not understand how He attained such power. And so, my heart filled with envy and anger. I secretly gathered other angels and asked them to bow to me. Some joined me. Others tried to dissuade me. But I would not relent."

He looked at Maryam sadly.

"Do you understand what I did to myself... and to those who followed me? I am forever cut off from Him. I can no longer behold Him, no longer bathe in His radiance. And I dragged my brethren down with me. I stripped them of the Creator's image and disfigured their angelic nature forever."

He fell silent, as if listening to his own words.

"You cannot understand this," he continued dully. "Bound in darkness for eternity, I had endless time to reflect. And you know what I realized, Maryam? It all began with you. With humans. Before you existed, we were happy. But this idea, to create the world and humanity—"

Maryam shook her head, feeling the cold seep into her bones.

"So, you regret what you did?" she asked quietly.

He looked at her with the eyes of one who had seen eternity, and smiled bitterly.

"No. I do not regret it."

"You are incurable," she said softly. "Pride and envy still rule you."

"Yes," he answered fiercely, turning sharply toward her. "And how could it be otherwise? I was His anointed Seraph. Other angels revered and praised me for my beauty and splendor."

The Dragon lifted his head, and for a fleeting instant, a celestial light flashed in his gaze.

"I was the head of music in Heaven, perhaps the most gifted musician among the angels. Can you imagine, Maryam, what it means to conduct the Divine Symphony, and suddenly hear a false note within it?"

"That note was me.

My doubt.

My desire to create in my own way."

He lowered his eyes, and darkness slid across his face like a living thing.

"Since then, I no longer hear the music of Heaven," he said quietly. "Only echoes. And even those are painful."

"Yes, I can see that," Maryam smiled wearily. "It's 'I, I, I' everywhere with you..."

She sighed softly, gathered her courage, and looked him straight in the eyes.

"Tell me, what do you all want from me?"

She reminded herself silently of who stood before her.

No matter how pitiful he seems, remember: before you stand the father of lies, the most ancient deceiver.

For a moment, he froze, as if her words pierced his ancient essence. His eyes, usually cold and bottomless, now reflected a strange vulnerability.

"What do we want from you?" he repeated slowly. "You do not yet understand your true purpose. You are the key, Maryam. The key to something that can change everything."

"Change..." she echoed with a bitter smile. "What can I change? Your defeat is already written in the tablets of the covenant."

He began to circle her slowly.

"Defeat?" he said softly. "Oh no, child. I never considered my fall a defeat. It was a choice. A conscious choice of a path that allowed me to see what is hidden from the eyes of Light."

"Nothing can be hidden from the Light," she whispered.

"And what did you see there?" she asked. "Eternal darkness and loneliness?"

He stopped directly in front of her, so close she felt his icy breath.

"I saw the truth, Maryam. A truth the Light tries to conceal. The Creator made us, but He did not give us free will. We were merely marionettes. Humans, however, were given freedom of choice."

"There is always a choice," she said quietly. "Even you had the choice to remain faithful."

The Dragon laughed, and his laughter echoed across the wasteland.

Choice?"

"Oh yes, there was a choice," his eyes flared with fire. "But at what cost? To become part of a system where everything is predetermined? Where is there no room for freedom? Where even love is nothing more than a component of a divine plan?"

Maryam remained silent—not because she had no answer, but because she understood that behind his distorted logic lay a lie, skillfully wrapped in the deceptive packaging of truth.

"You're simply continuing to convince yourself," she finally said. "But I see the truth. You were afraid of responsibility—and you chose the path of destruction."

His eyes blazed.

"Responsibility?"

"Oh yes, I was afraid," he admitted fiercely. "Afraid of being part of a world where doubt has no place, where there is no free will. Where even angels are merely instruments in the Creator's hands."

"And now what?" she asked quietly. "What do you want from me?"

"I need you," he said. "To be set free."

"How?" she whispered.

"You will renounce the Creator for my sake," he said with terrifying calm. "You will sacrifice yourself—just as Yeshua once sacrificed

Himself. But He offered Himself for humanity. You will offer yourself for me."

Maryam went pale.

"And my son?" she asked. "What will happen to him—and to the other children?"

"We will take care of them."

"How?"

"When you fulfill your destiny, a new world order will begin. The world will change. A new era will dawn. You need not worry about your son."

She shook her head slowly.

"I don't believe you. How can an order come through you? The world has only one true Ruler—the Highest. And how do you intend to bypass Him?"

"You will change everything," he said softly. "The Creator will continue to rule the worlds—but I will change. And perhaps I will be forgiven, at the price of your sacrifice. Just as all sinners were once forgiven through the sacrifice of Yeshua."

"But I am not Yeshua!" she cried. "I am nowhere near Him. I am only a sinful human being."

"Yes," he replied quietly, "you are a sinful human, but with a vast soul and a pure heart."

For a moment, he lowered his gaze.

"You pitied me, Maryam. You pitied a fallen Angel."

"How am I supposed to sacrifice myself?" she asked, her voice trembling.

"I think that is enough for today," he said calmly. "Dawn is near... You are exhausted."

Suddenly, Maryam realized he was right. She was unbearably tired, so tired that her legs could no longer support her, and her head felt as though it might split apart from pain. She swayed.

He caught her effortlessly, as if she weighed nothing at all.

And darkness closed in.

CHAPTER 19
INITIATION INTO MASTERY

She came to her senses in her room.

Light filtered through the thin curtains, gently sliding across the walls. Just as before, Aina was sitting beside her, watching her with quiet concern.

“At last, Maryam,” the girl said with relief. “You’re awake. Oh, these fainting spells of yours! You hardly eat anything at all, do you? You’re so fragile...” she fussed, unable to hide her joy at seeing Maryam conscious again.

“Aina... you’re here?” Maryam whispered weakly and smiled. “I’m so glad to see you. Tell me, dear Aina, how long was I asleep this time?”

“One day,” the girl replied.

“A whole day?” Maryam murmured. “That’s a long time... though compared to last time, it’s less. That’s a good sign.”

She smiled faintly, feeling her awareness slowly return.

At that moment, the door opened soundlessly, and Saman entered the room. Seeing Maryam sitting up, he exclaimed with exaggerated delight:

“Maryam! You’re awake? Wonderful! Your strength is returning at an astonishing rate—only one day of recovery! That’s truly impressive. Well done. Now you must eat properly.”

Without waiting for a reply, he turned to Aina.

"Aina! Bring her meat broth, strong coffee, and chocolate."

"Yes, sir," Aina replied, bowing, and hurried out.

Saman sat down on the edge of the bed.

"Maryam, the time has come to make a choice," he began seriously. "Tomorrow you will be expected in the ceremonial hall. The ritual will take place there. I am counting on your good sense and sincerely hope you won't arrange any... surprises. Everything must proceed smoothly."

Horror flickered across Maryam's face.

"Tomorrow? So soon? But I... I'm not ready. I don't have the strength."

"That can be remedied," he whispered.

His fingers closed around her hands, his gaze burning straight through her. An otherworldly bliss swept over her entire being; hot waves ran from her heels to the crown of her head. She barely managed to whisper:

"Lord, have mercy..."

Before a bright flash flared between them, and a warm, quiet grace poured into her chest. When she lifted her calm gaze to Saman, his face was twisted with rage. He sprang up and, without a word, stormed out, slamming the door behind him.

"Well... that was something," she thought. "I really do feel stronger."

She had no appetite at all.

Maryam went to the window and sank to her knees. She could not tell how long she prayed; time seemed to lose all meaning. When she finished, Aina was standing in the doorway, gazing at her in awe.

"Maryam, forgive me... I knocked, but you didn't hear me. I came in, and there was such light coming from you that I couldn't look away. You're so beautiful."

"Oh, Aina, thank you," Maryam smiled. "I didn't notice you come in—I felt so peaceful."

"Yes, Maryam," the girl said reverently. "I saw it. You... you were glowing like an angel. But now you really must eat."

"Aina, my dear, thank you—but I truly don't want to eat. I feel so well right now."

The girl lifted her eyes sadly.

"I understand. You look like an angel—your eyes are shining. But if you refuse the food, Saman will punish me. He doesn't like it when you disobey his orders."

Maryam thought for a moment, then smiled slightly, mischievously.

"Aina, what if we trick him and throw the meat outside? There are plenty of crows out there—they'll take care of it quickly. You can keep the chocolate and coffee for yourself."

"Maryam! You'd really throw away the meat?"

"Yes, Aina. And I don't advise you to eat it either. Think about it—what kind of meat is this? Have you ever seen livestock around here?"

Aina frowned.

"No... I haven't."

"Exactly," Maryam said with disgust. "Who knows whose meat ends up on our plates."

"Oh!" Aina gasped. "You're right—I never even thought of that."

"I don't want to eat their meat anymore either. But I'll gladly take the coffee and chocolate," she said, helping herself enthusiastically.

She had barely finished when there was a knock at the door, and Saman entered again. Maryam was just clearing away the empty plate where the appetizing steak had been. His gaze swept over the table and lingered on her. For a moment, approval flickered in his eyes—then was instantly replaced by suspicion.

"Aina, leave," he ordered curtly, without looking away from Maryam.

His tone was so commanding that the girl flinched and hurried out. When the door closed, Saman sat down, continuing to study Maryam intently.

"You never cease to amaze me."

"Why?" she asked, shivering under his gaze.

"You're literally glowing," he replied, leaning forward slightly.

Maryam looked at him in silence, trying to understand what lay behind his words. In his eyes, admiration warred with irritation, as if he were both captivated and unsettled by her.

"What exactly surprises you?" she finally asked.

"Your ability to resist. Your inner strength," he said. "It grows stronger every day, and that frightens me."

Maryam met his gaze.

"I'm not afraid of what I believe in," she said quietly.

A tense silence filled the room.

Saman stood, walked to the window, and froze, staring into the distance, as though speaking not to her, but to himself.

"Tomorrow will change everything," he said at last. "And your choice will determine far more than your own fate."

Maryam tensed.

"Tell me more about this ritual. What does it mean?"

Saman turned back to her. Something like regret flickered in his eyes.

"You'll learn in due time. " And for now..." he paused, "...let me give you one piece of advice: trust the process." Sometimes the path to truth runs through darkness."

Without waiting for an answer, he left the room, leaving Maryam alone with her thoughts.

She stepped up to the mirror and studied her reflection. Her eyes truly glowed with an inner light, and her skin seemed to radiate a soft, living shimmer.

At that moment, the door creaked open softly, and Aina slipped into the room. She froze on the threshold, nervously clasping her hands. Her eyes revealed a clear desire to say something, yet she seemed unable to find the strength to begin. Finally, gathering her courage, she whispered:

"Maryam, I heard him talking about tomorrow..." Her voice trembled with anxiety. "Maybe we should run away, while there's still time?"

Maryam looked at her thoughtfully.

"Aina, my dear... There is nowhere for me to run. My son is here. And the other children, the ones I must save."

Aina lowered her eyes.

"I know secret passages that lead beyond this place. But I'm afraid."

"Aina! Why didn't you say anything sooner?" Maryam exclaimed in a hushed voice. "I've been breaking my head trying to figure out how to get the children out. Tell me everything—or better yet, draw me a map. Only... where would we get a pencil and paper?"

"I have them," Aina said, pulling a small notebook and pencil from her pocket. "They gave them to me so I wouldn't forget things."

She began to sketch quickly. It turned out that beneath the ground lay an entire city, labyrinths, tunnels, and shafts. Without a map, escaping would be nearly impossible.

"And every exit is guarded," Aina continued. "But that can be handled. I know the cook—I can slip a sleeping draught into the guards' food."

"Aina," Maryam said gravely, looking straight into her eyes, "do you understand how much you're risking by helping us?"

"Yes, Maryam. I understand. But I don't want to live like this anymore. Today, when I saw you, so radiant, so beautiful, I realized how wonderful the Light truly is. I don't want to live in darkness."

“Thank you, Aina,” Maryam said softly. “May the Most High protect you, and may the angels watch over you.”

She paused, then added: “Now we must think through what to do if everything goes wrong. In that case, you must take the children and run without me.”

Maryam carefully explained how to reach Khalid, and then the city beyond the Wall. Aina, in turn, described every underground detail she knew.

“Let’s agree on this,” Maryam said. “If everything goes according to plan, you’ll come to me at midnight.”

They had barely finished speaking when the door flew open, and Saman entered without knocking.

He looked at Aina, and she immediately darted out of the room.

“Maryam,” he said, his voice dangerously calm, “I can feel it, you’re plotting something. Understand this: if you dare attempt anything, you will lose your son.”

Maryam met his gaze, though inside everything turned to ice.

“Saman, what could I possibly do?” she replied calmly. “You’ve bound me in chains by taking my son from me. Don’t worry, I’m not going anywhere.”

He stepped so close that his towering shadow engulfed her, as if trying to swallow her whole. It seemed to wrap around her, seeping inside. Breathing became difficult, and Maryam pressed herself against the wall. He placed his hand on her neck.

“What a delicate, slender neck,” he whispered, sliding his finger from the back of her jaw down her throat. “Right here is the carotid artery. If I press just a little harder—” he pressed slightly, “—you’ll lose consciousness. And if I press harder still, you'll die. Everything is in my hands," he said, staring at her with burning intensity.

Her breathing became ragged. He gently stroked her face. She began to suffocate. In her mind, the image of her Teacher appeared.

"Lord, help me," she whispered.

The spell broke.

He stepped back.

"Don't play games with me, Maryam," he said coldly. "I know more about your plans than you think."

Something predatory flashed in his eyes, and for a moment it seemed as though he could see straight through her.

"You have time until tomorrow," he continued, pacing the room in a slow circle. "Until the ritual. After that, everything will change. And not in your favor—if you continue to resist."

"I'm not afraid of you," she whispered barely audibly.

Saman stopped by the window, staring out into the dark courtyard.

"We'll see how long your courage lasts," he said over his shoulder and left, slamming the door behind him.

Maryam sank onto the bed, trying to gather her thoughts. Time was working against her—but there was no turning back. She had to save the children. She had to find her son.

A soft creak interrupted her thoughts. Like a shadow, Aina slipped into the room.

"He's gone?" she whispered.

"Gone," Maryam nodded. "But we can't waste time. The plan stands. By midnight, you must be ready."

Aina nodded. Her face was pale, but her resolve was firm.

"I won't let you down, Maryam. For the sake of the Light you carry, I'm ready for anything."

"Thank you, Aina," Maryam said, embracing her. The girl slipped out of the room.

With a heavy heart, Maryam sank to her knees in the middle of the room. Worry for Aina, for the fate of the children, for the success of their dangerous plan, all of it pressed heavily upon her soul. She remembered her Teacher's words:

"Do not resist. Surrender to the Creator. Let go, and everything will fall into place."

"Yes, Teacher," she whispered. "That's exactly what I will do... I surrender to the Creator."

"O Most High," she prayed softly, "hear my prayer and behold our suffering...

Forgive those who have strayed from the true path—for they do not know what they are doing. Deprived of Your Light, they wander in darkness, unable to find peace.

If it is Your will to receive my soul, I accept it with gratitude and humility.

But, O Merciful One, if there is still a way to save the innocent children, my son, and this world drowning in darkness, grant me that chance.

Enlighten them, Lord, and grant them forgiveness. Even in the darkest moments, I cannot stop pitying them, for there is no Light in their souls to lead them to the truth."

Her words, like the wings of angels, filled the room with a quiet radiance.

In that moment, Maryam felt an unfamiliar luminous force flowing into her, not the kind born of magic or sorcery, but one arising from sincere faith and love for others.

Suddenly, the air in the room thickened, saturated with a powerful presence.

She opened her eyes and saw, bathed in golden light, the figure of Arizal standing before her.

"Maryam," he said gently, "your hour has come. Remember everything I have taught you.

There is no time and no space. In moments of trial, by the Name of the Creator, you will be able to open any door."

Next, within the rays of Light, Michael appeared. His presence filled the space with calm strength.

"Your faith is your shield," he said firmly. "Do not doubt for a single moment."

The third to step into the circle of Light was Khalid.

"Maryam, my daughter," his voice sounded warm, almost fatherly, "you are a Warrior of the Light. You carry within you a great power, one that has now fully awakened."

Together, the three formed a glowing circle around her. Their voices merged into an ancient chant, sending waves of warmth and light through her body.

Arizal raised his hands above her head.

"Accept your true nature, Maryam. You are a Guardian of the Light.

All that exists is Light and desire. Desire draws Light; this is the eternal law of the universe.

Remember: there is nothing but the Creator."

Michael touched her forehead.

"Maryam, receive this Cup of Wisdom."

Upon his hand sat a great owl, holding a chalice filled with precious stones in its talons. He released the owl; it took flight, circled the room, and gently settled upon her head.

"May the wisdom of the ancients flow through your veins. Know this: power without love is nothing.

Remember the three youths who entered the blazing furnace."

He slipped a small red book into her pocket.

Khalid placed his hand upon her chest.

"Maryam, only through love and forgiveness will you overcome the darkness.

You are Light within the night, the voice of reason in chaos.

I consecrate you as a Master. From this moment on, you are one of us, and your task is to fight against the forces of Darkness."

At that instant, Maryam felt something immense awaken within her. Her consciousness expanded, granting her access to knowledge she had never known existed.

Arizal extended his ancient Black Book toward her.

"Now you will be able to read it. Your vessel is ready to contain this knowledge."

She accepted the book and immediately felt her bond with her Teacher deepen.

"Maryam, the time has come," their united voices echoed.

"We are always near, even when you cannot see us."

Their forms dissolved into the air and vanished.

CHAPTER 20
THE ESCAPE

THE RITE OF RENUNCIATION

Maryam opened her eyes.

Her entire being was filled with a quiet, luminous joy. Slowly, her consciousness cleared, returning her to reality.

Ayna will come soon... It's time to get ready, she thought.

A soft rustle came from behind the door — someone was carefully scratching, trying not to make a sound. Maryam went over and opened it slightly.

Ayna stood on the threshold, dressed in a warm jacket, sturdy boots, and a light knit hat.

"Maryam — I'm ready," the girl said firmly.

"Ayna, you were quick. Wait, I'll be right—"

Maryam opened the wardrobe, but there was no warm clothing inside.

"Hm... Someone was very thoughtful — making sure I couldn't leave the room without freezing."

Ayna smiled mysteriously.

"Maryam, I took care of that," she said, pulling an extra set of warm clothes from her backpack.

"Ayna, you're a miracle! How did you manage this? Where did you get all of this?" Maryam asked, hugging her with gratitude.

"It's a long story," Ayna waved it off. "Now isn't the time. We need to hurry. Get dressed."

"And the children?" Maryam asked anxiously. "They don't have warm clothes either."

Ayna silently nodded toward a second backpack.

"I took care of the children, too."

Unable to contain herself, Maryam rushed to her and embraced her tightly.

"May the Lord bless you for your kindness!"

Ayna grew shy and looked away.

"Maryam, we really must hurry."

"Yes, of course. But before we go, let us pray. The road ahead is long and dangerous. May the Almighty strengthen our hearts and grant us wisdom in the trials to come."

Maryam knelt, and Ayna joined her. Their shared prayer steadied them, filling them with calm resolve.

They rose and moved toward the exit.

"Ayna, how will we get through there?"

"Don't worry. There's no one there now. They trust me."

She carefully stepped into the corridor.

"It's clear. Come," she whispered, taking Maryam's hand and pulling her in the opposite direction from the lit hallway, toward what Maryam had thought was a solid stone wall.

Ayna stopped at an old section of masonry, darkened with age. Her fingers traced the stone, searching for something almost invisible.

A soft click.

Part of the wall slid aside, revealing a dark passage.

"Here," Ayna whispered, stepping into the darkness first.

Maryam followed.

Inside, the air was heavy and damp, thick with the smell of earth and time. Ayna pulled a small flashlight from her pocket, its beam illuminating rough stone steps.

The deeper they descended, the colder it became. They exchanged glances, shivering involuntarily.

Maryam, feeling the anxiety rise, stopped and hugged the girl.

"Ayna..." her voice trembled. "Thank you for everything. May the Lord protect you."

Ayna opened her mouth to reply, but suddenly a distant noise echoed from deep within the tunnel.

"Are they chasing us? Run!" she cried, grabbing Maryam's hand and pulling her forward.

"Ayna, wait — let's split up. That gives us a better chance."

Ayna turned. The flashlight lit her pale face.

"Maryam... are you sure? What if you get lost?"

"Don't worry. I have the map."

Ayna hesitated.

"Are you certain? If you lose the map and get lost, it's almost impossible to get out."

"I'll manage... with God's help. The map is in my head. We'll meet at the hangar. Don't wait for me — if I'm delayed, gather the children and get them outside."

"And you?" Ayna asked, her voice shaking.

"I need to get my son. Everything will be fine," Maryam said softly, forcing a smile.

"Go. God willing, we'll meet at Khalid's place, or beyond the Wall."

They embraced. Ayna sobbed once, then ran in the opposite direction, leaving her spare flashlight behind.

Maryam took a deep breath, whispered a prayer, and moved down the dark corridor, holding the map in her mind.

In the dim light, shadows danced along the walls. Strange sounds echoed somewhere nearby. At times, muffled moans drifted through the tunnels, sending a chill down her spine.

Suddenly, a barrier loomed before her.

Wait. Stop.

If I didn't make a mistake — and I couldn't have — the map shows a straight passage here. Where did this wall come from?

Maryam pulled out the map to check — just as the flashlight flickered... and went out.

“No... no, no... not now,” she groaned in despair.

She shook the flashlight. Useless.

In frustration, she threw it to the ground and froze.

“Lord, please help me,” Maryam whispered, moving her hands along the wall — until she realized she was walking in circles.

Something was wrong.

“Lord, help me,” she whispered again.

And then — behind her — a commanding voice rang out...

— Not at all. And let Aina go with them.

Aina? — he burst out laughing. — She betrayed you. Haven’t you realized that yet? She was assigned to you for that very purpose.

That doesn’t matter, — Maryam whispered. — I forgive her. And I want you to honor my terms.

The Head turned sharply.

Zar. Bring Aina.

Zar bowed and left. Moments later, he returned, dragging a sobbing girl with him.

The Head rose and stepped toward her.

Why are you crying? — his voice was deceptively gentle.

Aina trembled, unable to lift her head. Tears streamed down her face.

Zar.

His expression darkened; his gaze turned opaque and cold.

You failed to purge this sentimentality from her. You're a poor mentor.

Forgive me... — Zar muttered, lowering his head. — She was changing, but Maryam's Light... it affected her badly.

Light?! — The Head roared. — How dare you speak to me of Light here?

I'll fix it! She'll be fixed! She already is—by betraying Maryam and the children!

What are you talking about? Look at her. Guilt is tearing her apart.

The Head turned slowly toward Zar. His voice dropped to a glacial whisper, final as a sentence:

You have failed. I no longer require your services.

Horror flooded Zar's face.

But I served you faithfully! He screamed. It's her fault!

Rage ignited in his eyes. Unable to restrain himself, he lunged at Maryam.

The Head merely lifted his hand.

Zar froze mid-motion.

His body petrified instantly, as though it had been turned to stone. Only his eyes—wide with terror- continued to roll in their sockets.

The Head stepped closer, ran his palm over Zar's head, then seized him by the hair and, with a single brutal motion, tore it off.

Zar's body collapsed, still twitching in convulsions. His eyes continued to stare, spinning wildly, as if unable to comprehend what had happened.

That's all, — the Head said calmly. Human life is worth nothing.

He snapped his fingers. Sparks flew from his hand. The severed head ignited and crumbled into ash across the floor.

Aina, he called. Clean this up.

Aina went pale. Her lips trembled. She took a step forward, swayed, and collapsed silently, losing consciousness.

The Head didn't even glance at her.

He circled Maryam like a predator studying its prey.

Do you see now, Maryam? His voice was almost casual. Resistance is pointless. Everything is already decided.

He walked over to Aina and touched her lightly.

She gasped, shuddered, and looked up at him in confusion. Then memory returned—she recoiled, breaking into soundless sobs.

Stop it, he hissed. Stand up.

Shaking, Aina forced herself to her feet.

You'll be taken to the children. Gather them and leave.

Then he turned back to Maryam.

Are your demands satisfied?

I want to see everything you're releasing. All the children. All the adults.

The Head narrowed his eyes.

Careful, Maryam. Don't cross the line.

Her chest tightened as though clamped in iron. She silently called out to God. Warmth slowly replaced the cold spreading through her body.

The Head glared at her, his patience thinning.

Your distrust displeases me.

Forgive me, she said evenly. It isn't distrust. It's caution.

He stopped directly in front of her.

Caution, you say? He repeated mockingly. How fascinating. You grow more amusing by the moment.

He snapped his fingers. Several figures in dark cloaks appeared.

Take Aina to the children, he ordered. Make sure they leave the grounds.

Still trembling, Aina stepped toward the exit, then turned back, searching Maryam's eyes for reassurance.

Maryam nodded faintly.

As for your request, the Head continued, never taking his eyes off Maryam, I will grant it.

He clapped his hands.

The air shimmered. Before them, unfolded a scene like a vast screen: men, women, children standing in groups, some held hands. Some stood silent, bewildered.

Look, said the Head. They are free. Every one of them has been given a chance at a new life.

Maryam studied their faces carefully, searching for deception, fear, pain, anything that would betray illusion.

They looked confused... but alive.

Satisfied? he asked.

Yes, she replied, though doubt still churned inside her. But how can I be sure nothing will happen to them once they leave?

The Head laughed.

Maryam, Maryam... he drawled. Your suspicion is almost touching. Believe me: those granted freedom are of no further interest to me. They are truly free.

Very well, she said, masking her distrust beneath calm submission. — I hope you keep your word.

He tilted his head slightly, studying her.

What surprises me most, Maryam, is that you never once asked about your son. Do the lives of strangers matter more to you than your own child?

She met his gaze calmly, exhaled, then lowered her eyes. Gathering strength, she spoke:

No, Head. I worry deeply for my son. But others need help too. Would God hear me if my concern extended only to those closest to me? God reveals Himself through the suffering and the needy. And if I wish to see Him here, on this earth, I must look into the eyes of everyone who cries out for help.

Nonsense. Everything you say is utter nonsense. He is not here on this earth.

Look around you: the land is filled with the needy. And in each of them, you claim to see Him? he laughed, staring straight into her eyes.

Tell me, Head, she interrupted his mockery. — Where is my son?

He paused, savoring the moment.

Your son is here, he said slowly, drawing out every word.

Here?! Maryam cried out. Where?

You will see him immediately after the rite of renunciation.

What kind of rite is that?

You will renounce Him and bow before me.

Bow before you? You keep demanding this of me. Why?

Do not ask unnecessary questions. Do what you must. I have already wasted too much time on you.

Time? — She raised her brows in quiet astonishment. — Of all beings, you should know that time and space are illusions.

For a split second, irritation flashed in his eyes.

Do not test my patience, Maryam, — he said coldly, barely restraining himself. — I fulfilled all your demands. You have fulfilled none.

He stepped closer.

You are a liar.

Maryam said nothing. Her mind raced, searching desperately for a way to buy time—time for Aina and the children to get farther away.

Head... may I see my son? — She asked almost submissively.

Of course.

He turned sharply and barked:

Saman! Bring the boy!

"Lord, save and protect us," Maryam prayed fervently, clasping her hands.

Saman vanished. Less than five minutes later, he returned, leading a boy by the arm.

A mother's heart clenched in agony as she longed to rush to him, to wrap him in her arms, to shield him from this nightmare.

Here is your child, Maryam, — the Head declared triumphantly. — Now bow. Acknowledge me as your master!

Mama! Mommy, don't do it! I'm not afraid of them! — The boy cried out, though fear gleamed in his eyes. He was terrified—not for himself, but for her.

The Head narrowed his eyes.

You've poisoned his mind well, he hissed. Even we couldn't purge him of this... delusion about your God. Very well.

So, you are not afraid? He said thoughtfully and snapped his fingers.

At once, two figures in dark cloaks appeared from nowhere. They seized the boy by the arms and dragged him toward the adjoining hall.

Maryam lunged forward instinctively, but the Head stopped her with a single commanding gesture.

Do not rush. There is no need, he smiled. No time and no space—your words, not mine.

As for me, I'll tell you this: we have all eternity ahead of us.

He relished the fear in her eyes.

Trembling, Maryam placed her hand in his. Matching his pace, she followed him into the next hall, whispering prayers without pause.

They entered a vast chamber.

The dogs bared their teeth the instant they saw them. The fire in the hearth flared brighter.

The cloaked figures dragged the boy closer to the flames. The searing heat scorched the hem of his clothes. The smell of burned hair filled the air.

It was clear the heat was unbearable, yet he endured it silently, looking at his mother while tears streamed down her face.

The Head loomed above them all, darker than the shadows themselves.

He snapped his fingers again.

The fire roared higher.

The boy squeezed his eyes shut. Tears burst from them as he screamed from the pain:

"Lord! Heavenly Father! Save my mother and me!"

At once, the dogs snarled and stepped forward, ready to leap.

Maryam! The Head's voice thundered. Bow before me! Or your son will burn alive in this infernal fire!

Every fiber of Maryam's being shook with terror for her child.

And yet, to everyone's astonishment, she spoke calmly:

No, Head. I will not bow to you.

I believe in the One God alone,

Creator of heaven and earth, of all that is seen and unseen.

To Him alone do I bow.

She lifted her gaze.

And you...

Begone from me, Satan.

The Head's face twisted with inhuman fury. His features darkened, his eyes flooded with blood, veins bulging at his temples like thick cords.

"Seize them!" he roared. "Throw them both into the fire!"

The guards lunged forward, grabbing Maryam and her son. The child's scream, raw with terror and despair, pierced her heart like a blade.

In that instant, something shattered deep within a mother's soul and at once ignited with unimaginable force.

With sudden ferocity, Maryam tore herself free from the guards' grip, stunning them with her resolve, and rushed toward the Head. No one had expected this. The entire hall froze, unsure how to react.

She stopped at the center of the chamber, drew a deep breath, and closed her eyes. Whispering a prayer, Maryam felt a surge of heat rise within her chest. Three times she spoke the sacred Name of God. Slowly, she raised her hands, gathering threads of fiery energy that had been accumulating within her for years, drawing them upward from the depths of her being.

Her entire body vibrated as if connected to a high-voltage current, filling with blinding light. The air around her quivered, condensing into a vast, radiant sphere. With the Name of God on her lips, Maryam hurled the sphere toward the Head.

Like living lightning, it struck his chest and hurled him across the hall, smashing him into the far wall.

Exhausted, Maryam collapsed to her knees. Her son ran to her, wrapped his arms around her, and helped her rise.

"Mom... are you okay?" he whispered, breathless with fear.

"Yes, my love," she said through tears, pulling him close and kissing his beloved eyes.

"Bravo," came a cold voice behind them.

They flinched.

Maryam froze, then slowly turned. A few steps away stood the Head, clapping slowly, mockingly.

"Maryam," he said, feigning admiration, "your power is truly impressive."

She stood, instinctively shielding her son with her body.

"Listen," she said, steadying her voice. "As I recall, a sacrifice must be voluntary. Otherwise, this whole spectacle loses its meaning."

He burst out laughing.

"A spectacle, you say?" Madness flashed in his eyes.

"Ah, Maryam," he continued calmly, "you are absolutely right. A sacrifice must indeed be voluntary. But here is the problem, you turned out to be a liar."

He stepped closer.

"You were supposed to bow the moment I released the children. Instead, you deceived me. But then again, you are just like all humans."

"Apparently not quite," she said quietly with a faint smile. "Since my bow seems so important to you. And for the record, I never promised to bow. I said I would make a deal."

"Do not play with me," he hissed. "Or else—"

"Or else what?" she interrupted calmly. "I'm standing right here. If you truly wanted me dead, I would have been long gone. But you need me for something else. So perhaps we can still negotiate."

"Enough!" His eyes flared with fire. "There is nothing left to discuss. I kept my side of the bargain. The children are free. Now it's your turn. Bow willingly, or I will force you, by inflicting pain on both of you."

His gaze slid toward the boy, and Maryam barely suppressed a shudder.

"Why do you need this?" she asked, masking her fear with deliberate confusion.

“Enough!” he thundered. “No more bargains. You are playing with the devil’s tail. All that is required of you is to bow and renounce your Master.”

“He is not my master,” she whispered. “He is my Father.”

“What difference does it make?” he sneered. “You were slaves, and slaves you will die.”

“Oh, for heaven’s sake,” Maryam scoffed. “Bow, bow, bow. Narcissist.”

He paused, then smiled slowly.

“I hear everything, Maryam. And you know what? I agree. Why not? We have been granted unlimited power over this world. And you humans deserve it. For a thousand days now, I have enjoyed this authority. People across the world have bowed to me because they had no choice.”

He spoke reverently, almost devoutly.

“Oh, there is a choice, of course. Those who bow receive everything: food, water, and medicine. The rest are condemned to starve. Those who refuse me lose all rights. Most of humanity lacked the strength to give up earthly comforts. Humans are pitiful, weak creatures. But I will heal this world. In my world, where they accept me, there will be no sickness, no suffering, no loss. And I offer you a role in this correction. Be part of it.”

“Of course,” Maryam said thoughtfully. “There will be no sick, because you’ll simply destroy them. And you’ll mutilate the souls of the rest.”

"Maryam, what pessimism," he said sarcastically. "I'm not mutilating anyone. Humans have long mutilated themselves. That is their flawed nature."

Suddenly, his mood shifted violently.

"Enough! No more empty words! Are you ready to bow?"

His voice thundered with such force that Maryam's insides trembled, goosebumps racing across her skin.

"Bow! Accept my mark! You have no choice!"

He moved dangerously close to the boy. The child clutched her hand, pressing into her.

Maryam swallowed the lump in her throat and hoarsely whispered:

"The Lord is my light and my salvation, whom shall I fear?"

"So that's how it is?" he growled.

"Saman! Take the boy. Put him on the table."

Saman appeared, seized the trembling child, lifted him like a reed, and laid him on the stone table. The boy stared at his mother as his hands were bound. Silent. Terrified.

"Look, Maryam!" the Head shouted. "Is this what you wanted?!"

He raised his arms and murmured words unknown. His body convulsed, his eyes bloodshot, his beautiful face contorted.

"Maryam! This is your last chance. Bow to me and acknowledge me, or there will be no turning back!"

Maryam closed her eyes and spoke words stronger than any weapon:

"You shall worship the Lord your God, and Him alone shall you serve."

The Head recoiled, glaring at her with pure hatred.

"You have drained the last drop of my patience," he trembled with rage, extending his hands toward her.

The knife that had rested peacefully on the table rose as if alive and floated into her palm. She tried desperately to open her fingers, but they would not obey. Her legs carried her forward against her will, toward her son.

Another second, and she stood above him, arm raised, knife poised.

"Mom, don't!" the boy screamed.

His cry struck her like lightning, tearing her from paralysis. The dragon's words echoed in her memory:

"Like a lamb he will go to slaughter, and you will be powerless."

"I will not!" she cried.

"Head, you think yourself all-powerful, but that is a lie! The One God is the only true power in this world. And you are nothing but an illusion!"

Speaking the sacred four-letter Name, she tore through the unseen spell. The air shuddered. Light flooded the space. The darkness binding her shattered.

Her body obeyed her again.

She freed her son and pulled him close.

"Mom..." he sobbed. "I was so scared. You were like... like a zombie."

She stroked his hair and kissed his forehead.

“Don’t be afraid, my love. The Lord will not abandon us.”

She looked up and froze.

The hall was empty.

No Head. No Saman. No guards.

“It was an illusion,” she realized, gripping her son’s hand. “We have to find a way out.”

But it was not easy. They searched the hall—no doors, no exits. Nothing.

“Are we trapped?” the boy whispered.

“There is a way,” she said softly, recalling her teacher’s words.

“We simply cannot see it. There is no time and no space.”

She closed her eyes.

“Then we must step beyond space itself.”

CHAPTER 21

THE REPENTANCE OF THE FALLEN

"If therefore the light that is in thee be darkness, how great is that darkness!"

— Matthew 6:23 (KJV)

Maryam closed her eyes and sank to her knees.

The boy followed without a word. They prayed in silence, holding tightly to one another's hands.

When she opened her eyes again, something caught her attention—a narrow recess in the wall. Strange. She was certain it had not been there before. Gently, she tugged her son's hand and stepped closer. Deep within the stonework, barely visible in the dim light, she could make out the faint outline of a door.

"Here," she whispered.

The door yielded at the slightest touch.

Beyond it lay the familiar hall with the fireplace. A gentle fire crackled in the hearth, filling the air with warmth and the scent of woodsmoke. It was hard to believe that only moments ago, this place had seemed like the very gates of hell.

Maryam looked around slowly. The chairs. The stone walls. The steady glow of the hearth. Everything appeared peaceful—almost inviting.

And yet something was wrong.

"Where did they all go?" she whispered.

The silence felt artificial, like a stage set hastily rearranged between scenes.

Then a strange rustling sound came from above.

The boy flinched and pressed closer to his mother.

They looked up.

The massive chandelier shaped like a dragon began to move.

Before their eyes, the creature came alive. Like a colossal serpent, it unwound itself in enormous coils, sliding downward from the ceiling. In the next instant, a towering being stood before them—ancient, immense, breathing as though time itself moved through its lungs.

"Greetings, Maryam," the dragon's voice resounded—low and cavernous, as though echoing from the depths of a mountain. "I am glad to see you again. I have been watching you. You have done remarkably well."

His attention shifted toward the boy. Swaying with exhaustion, he nevertheless forced himself to stand straight. A faint, almost amused expression touched the dragon's face.

"You were brave," he said. "Though it hasn't been an easy day for you."

“I won’t give you my mother!” the boy burst out, clenching his fists.

“Brave,” the dragon replied calmly. “Your mother has raised you well. But now you must rest.”

He made the slightest movement with one claw. The fire in the hearth softened, glowing warmer and gentler. A high-backed chair draped with a thick woollen blanket appeared beside it.

The boy blinked. Fatigue overtook him all at once. He sank into the chair—and within seconds, he was asleep.

“Do not worry,” the dragon said, noticing Maryam’s anxious glance. “He needs to regain his strength.”

He fell silent for a moment, as though weighing his words, then continued more quietly.

“The light you carry presses hard against the darkness.”

He gave a strained, humorless chuckle.

“Even the descendant of Dan could not withstand you…”

He shook his great head, still faintly amused.

“Arrogant creature. Always lecturing others about human weakness. Always judging. And yet… a descendant of a slave woman. That is where his hatred of humanity was born, isn’t it?”

For a long while, he stared into the flames. In his eyes flickered something deeper than mockery—an ancient, wounded sorrow in which weariness, bitterness, and longing were intertwined.

"You are under powerful protection," he said at last. "He Himself watches over you."

"And that is precisely why I require your freely chosen sacrifice."

Maryam stiffened.

"I need your help," the dragon continued. "Through your sacrifice, I may finally change... and perhaps receive forgiveness."

"You cannot imagine the centuries of longing that have consumed me," he said quietly. "I miss my brothers..."

"A voluntary sacrifice," Maryam repeated dryly.

"Especially after I was forced to nearly slit my own son's throat."

"That was a performance," he rasped, without threat, without anger.

"A performance?" she echoed.

"A performance where the audience is suddenly thrown into a bloody quest for survival? If you want forgiveness, then repent. The Lord is merciful. He will forgive you."

She met his eyes.

"Your request reminds me of a story about a great elder, Saint Anthony the Great."

And she began to tell the tale.

A demon named Zerepher once appeared before Saint Anthony to test whether God would accept a repentant demon. Disguised as a weeping man, he came before the elder.

God, wishing to show that He rejects no one who comes to Him, did not reveal the deception.

Anthony looked at him as an ordinary man and asked:

"Who are you, and what has happened to you that you weep so bitterly?"

"Holy Father," replied the demon,

"I am not a man, but a demon, evil, burdened with countless sins."

"What do you want of me?" Anthony asked, assuming humility.

"Nothing," said the demon, "except that you ask your God whether He would forgive me if I repented."

Anthony answered:

"Go home today. Return tomorrow, and I will give you His answer."

That night, the elder prayed fervently, asking whether God would accept one whose sins surpassed even those of demons.

Suddenly, an angel of the Lord appeared and said:

"This is what the Lord declares:

Why did you pray for a demon? He came to tempt you."

Anthony asked:

"Why did God not reveal this to me?"

The angel replied:

"God rejects no one who approaches Him—not even Satan himself.

When he comes again, tell him this: God turns away from no one. He will accept him if he does what God commands."

"But when he asks what he must do, tell him:

You are ancient evil. You are unyielding pride.

How can you repent?

If you truly desire forgiveness on the Day of Judgment, stand in one place for three years, day and night, facing east, and say:

'Lord, have mercy on me, ancient evil.'

And one hundred times say aloud: 'Have mercy on me, darkened deception.'

Only then will you be forgiven and restored among the angels."

The angel then ascended to heaven.

The next day, the demon returned, again disguised as a grieving man.

Anthony told him that God would accept his repentance if he obeyed.

"What must I do?" the demon asked.

Anthony repeated God's command.

The demon burst into loud laughter.

"If I wished to call myself ancient evil, darkened, cursed— I would have done so long ago and been saved instantly," he sneered.

"But now? Now I am clothed in glory.

All serve me. All fear me.

And now you ask me to call myself wretched?

To bow as a worthless servant?

No, old man. That will never be."

With a scream, the demon vanished.

Anthony fell to his knees and prayed:

"Truly, the angel spoke rightly, ancient evil does not become new goodness."

Maryam finished her story and looked expectantly at the dragon.

"I fear history is repeating itself," she said softly, smiling.

"I remember that story," he said, his eyes flashing.

"There was such a demon... He met a grim end," he added darkly.

"But this is not about them. This is about me.

"You do not understand, Maryam. I cannot simply repent. My nature, my very essence—"

"That is precisely why you must repent," Maryam interrupted him.

"Because your essence is what makes your choice so meaningful. You could become the one who proves that even the darkest being can find his way back to who he was created to be—to the Light."

The dragon froze. Conflicting emotions flickered in his eyes.

A heavy silence filled the hall, broken only by the crackle of burning logs.

"Do you truly think I am foolish enough to believe such naïve lies?" he growled, though uncertainty slipped into his voice.

"I think you are wise enough to recognize the truth," Maryam replied calmly.

“The truth is this: you have a choice. There is always a choice.”

“We have no choice!” he cried out. “And we never did!

You, humans, have a choice. We do not. From the moment of our creation, we were made to serve. And then, as it turned out, to serve you as well.

“The greatest insult was not that He created humanity. It was the prospect of submitting to it. That was the final straw.”

Bitterness filled his voice.

“My followers and I once held high rank in the heavenly hierarchy. We could not accept the idea of bowing to a creature formed only recently, from the dust of the earth, and, in our judgment, unworthy of such exalted authority.”

He fell silent, lost in memory.

“Before the fall, I was appointed to govern the earth. And the earth was formless and void, shrouded in darkness.

I was an Angel of Light. But severed from God, the Self-Existing, I became an Angel of Darkness. The earth sank deeper into shadow, and the angels I led were cast ‘under darkness,’ becoming rulers of this present age of night.”

His voice grew quieter, as if admitting guilt.

“From the beginning, it was ordained that I would become the chief warden of your world. By your deeds, humans are sent either to my prison or upward, to Him.”

A grim smile crossed his face.

"Your earthly justice mirrors ours. In your world, there are criminals, police, judges, and prisons. So, it is ours."

Lesser demons are assigned to criminals, recording their crimes and issuing penalties. You experience these as pain and loss.

If that is not enough, there is judgment and imprisonment.

"And what happens in your prisons is horrific. But it cannot compare to what occurs in ours.

"And over it all stands me.

"I was the Angel appointed as guardian of the world, by the Creator's own will. In my nature, there was once only purity and innocence.

Oh, how beautiful I was in my original glory!

"But pride, like poison, entered my being.

I, a daring disciple, desired to equal the Creator... to surpass my Teacher.

"And for that audacity, judgment followed.

"In my madness, I drew my subordinate angels after me, and a war broke out in Heaven.

Michael and his host stood against my followers and me. But the balance of power was not in our favor, and there was no place left for us in the heavenly courts.

Cast down, we found ourselves in the earthly realm."

He lifted his gaze.

“The hour of Judgment draws near. The time appointed for the eternal torment of the fallen angels approaches.

And the Creator will say: ‘Depart from Me, you accursed, into the eternal fire prepared for the devil and his angels.’

“That time is close—very close.

The hoofbeats of Dan’s riders are already heard. The earth is perishing. Cities lie in ruins. People destroy one another.

For a thousand days now, a descendant of Dan has ruled under my command. Time is running out.”

His voice sharpened.

“I need you, Maryam. Save me, and you will save the earth.

Otherwise, everything will vanish: the earth, humanity, life itself.”

Maryam listened, her heart aching.

How she longed to help humanity. And yet she pitied him, the one who had brought so much suffering into the world.

Despite all his crimes, all the horrors committed under his command—wars, violence, the pain inflicted on children, despite all of it...

He was an abyss of terror and darkness.

And yet, against all reason, her heart was filled with compassion for him.

Maryam sank to her knees.

At first, she could not speak at all.

Then, something within her broke open.

“Lord! Lord! Heavenly Father!” she cried.

“I beg You, forgive all the people of the earth and receive them into Your dwelling.

Lord, I ask You, forgive him. Lord, forgive!”

Tears streamed down her face. Her body filled with divine grace, shining with an unearthly light.

The dragon stared at her without blinking.

“You... prayed for me,” he said hoarsely.

“For the fallen one...

“I thank you, Maryam.

“Look...”

CHAPTER 22
THE CHOICE

In that very moment, the silence was pierced by the distinct sound of footsteps.

A heavy door creaked open, and a guard in a dark cloak entered the hall. Behind him, a man whose face was hidden beneath a deep hood followed.

Something about him felt unmistakably familiar: his gait, the way he held his shoulders, the very rhythm of his movement.

Maryam's heart froze with a sudden, aching premonition.

"Who is that?" she whispered, unable to hide her trembling.

The guard slowly pulled back the hood.

And time itself seemed to stop.

Before her stood her husband.

The face she had seen so many times in her dreams.

The same gaze, where strength and kindness once met. Only now he looked older, his eyes marked by a deep shadow, but still unmistakably him. Still her own.

The boy saw his father and let out a piercing cry before running forward.

"Dad! Daddy!" he shouted with joy.

The man dropped to his knees and wrapped his son in his arms.

The child's laughter rang through the hall, alive, radiant, pushing back the darkness, the fear, the long loneliness of this place.

Maryam rushed toward her husband, pressing herself against him, her tears falling freely, tears of disbelief and overwhelming joy.

"How is this possible?" she whispered, cupping his face as though afraid he might vanish.

"Where have you been all this time? Oh God... I'm so glad to see you."

"Maryam," he said, holding her tightly, as if to make sure she was real.

"Praise be to the Most High. You're alive. Every day I prayed for this, and He heard me."

He brushed her hair back gently, then looked at his son.

"There is so much I want to tell you... So much has happened. But not here. We must leave—now."

He raised his eyes toward the Dragon.

"Are we free to go?"

"Yes," came the cold reply. "I am letting you go. But not all of you.

Maryam must stay. She still has her choice to make."

"No!" the man cried out fiercely. "You cannot tear us apart again!"

He stepped forward, shielding Maryam and their son.

"Let me stay in her place! Do you hear me?! I will not leave my wife with you, spawn of darkness!"

"Silence!" the Dragon thundered, his voice echoing through the stone, cutting straight into the soul.

"No! You will not silence me," the man shouted back.

"And I will not let you take her again. Over my dead body!"

The Dragon laughed, bitter mockery in his voice.

"It is not for you to decide who lives and who dies," he said, and the fire in the hearth flared higher.

"You think this is your power?" the man roared, his fists clenched white.

"Only the Most High judges life and death. He alone decides who lives and who dies—not you. And if it is His will that I die, so be it, but you will not have Maryam."

In his cry lived everything at once: pain, rage, love, despair.

"Eli, stop! Please!" Maryam cried, grasping his hand and searching his eyes, as if trying to carve his face into her memory forever.

"How good it is that you are here. Please take our son and go. May the Lord protect you."

"No," he said firmly. "You are not staying here."

"Eli," she interrupted, her voice breaking into a whisper.

"You must do this. Stop thinking of yourself, or we will all perish. Think of our son."

He shook his head bitterly.

"Maryam... how can you say that?" he rasped.

"Do you think I'm thinking of myself?"

He looked at the boy, pale as death, staring at his father without blinking.

"Everything I do is for you. For him. For you."

"Enough!" the Dragon snarled.

"Eli, take the boy by the hand and say goodbye to your wife."

"No," the man said, gripping Maryam's hand. "I will not leave her."

"Maryam, my love," he said, trying to steady his voice.

"I searched for you for so long. Until I met people who said they knew where you and our son were. Then came long days in a prison cell. And now, at last, you are here with me. I cannot lose you again."

The hall fell silent.

Only the fire crackled, throwing restless shadows across the walls.

Maryam closed her eyes and slowly shook her head.

"There is no choice, Eli," she whispered.

"Do as he says. Take our son. Protect him."

"Maryam... I love you. And I will love you forever. Forgive me—but—"

He took the boy's hand and reached out to embrace her—

But before he could, the Dragon clapped his claws together.

And they were gone.

Maryam stood alone.

Horrified, she turned toward the Dragon.

“What have you done?” she cried through tears.

“Where are they? Where did you send them?”

“Do not worry, Maryam,” the Dragon said calmly.

“They are safe with your friends. Look.”

He snapped a claw, and a shimmering screen appeared before her, like an image in an old cinema.

She saw her husband and son standing beside Arizal and Michael, beyond the Wall, in Arizal’s city.

Maryam closed her eyes and exhaled in relief.

“Thank God... they are safe.”

She turned back to the Dragon.

Now he seemed immense, eight, perhaps ten meters tall. His form flickered in the firelight, as though shaped from darkness itself.

Only one thing she could not understand:

How could she look him straight in the eyes when he towered so far above her?

“Maryam,” the Dragon’s voice rolled through space itself, “there is neither time nor space. Time exists only on Earth. I can be here with you, and at the same moment, in thousands of other places. “I want you to see that the world is not black and white, as you believe. Behind every light there is a shadow, and within every shadow, light. A human comes to the Light by passing through Darkness. And even in every righteous soul, there are dark stains."

The Dragon's voice filled the hall, and it seemed as though the very air began to resonate. "As long as you are alive," he said, "You possess free will, and we possess the freedom to influence you. But if we did not exist, how would you ever accomplish your task and become righteous? You would revel in naked light alone, as one of your great writers once said. And he was right."

He leaned closer. His breath sent a shiver across her skin.

"I am Darkness," the Dragon continued,

"And you are Light. And only together can we heal the world. Here, at this point of intersection, where Light and Darkness meet, overturn one another, and become one whole, just as you once supposed."

His voice softened, almost human.

"You are my correction, Maryam. There is immense power within you. Change the world. Take up your cross and offer yourself as a sacrifice for it. But first... I want to show you something."

In the next instant, she felt the ground fall away beneath her feet.

"Look..."

He lifted her effortlessly, as though she weighed nothing at all.

"Close your eyes," the Dragon whispered.

She obeyed, and they ascended.

It was terrifying. Her body trembled with the immense force flowing through her.

And yet, at the same time, an indescribable rapture filled every cell of her being.

The sensations grew so vivid that reality itself dissolved. Maryam could not tell whether they were truly flying or whether her body was dissolving, merging with this living darkness. But her entire being surged upward, toward a single central point, the heart of the spiral of life.

“Open your eyes,” a voice sounded within her. “Look.”

She opened them.

Before her stretched a wondrous world.

Emerald forests rolled endlessly beneath a boundless azure sky. Every blade of grass, every leaf, shimmered as if dusted with diamond dew. Maryam soared above this unearthly beauty, and such joy flooded her soul that human language felt utterly inadequate to describe it.

Here, within this perfect world, she longed to dissolve completely, to remain forever, bathed in the unspeakable delight of the Creator.

But the Dragon’s voice broke her rapturous union with perfection.

“Maryam,” he said,

“You have earned this place. You may remain here; in this paradise I once knew. But there is a price. If you stay, the world will perish. Or you may return to Earth, where you must offer the greatest sacrifice. Through your death, you will save the world, and perhaps even me. Make your choice.”

Without hesitation, she answered:

“I will return to Earth.”

At once, the sun began to dim, then vanished entirely.

Light collapsed into a single, delicate thread, shrinking into a point, and disappeared.

Everything around her dissolved.

A dense, living darkness enveloped all, without up or down, without time or space. In that silence, she heard only the beating of her own heart, heavy, resonant, like the tolling of a bell.

"Remember," the Dragon's voice echoed from afar, as though through the weight of ages.

"Death is not the end. Death is the beginning."

EPILOGUE

The darkness dissolved, as though it had never existed.

Maryam found herself standing on the shore of a raging sea. Waves crashed violently against the coastal rocks, hurling white foam skyward. She stood there, unable to understand how she had arrived. The world around her looked like a living canvas, something straight out of a Levitan painting.

Suddenly, a voice thundered from the heavens, and the very fabric of space trembled:

“Maryam. Your hour has come. Take up your Cross, and the world will be saved. But know this: for you, this sacrifice will be the last.”

Fear rose sharply within her. When death stands before you face to face, terror slips into the soul like a cold, coiling serpent. Yet casting doubt aside, she stepped forward and entered the water.

The sea greeted her with a thousand splashes, as if creation itself longed to be cleansed through her.

And then, above the surface of the water, He appeared.

Within Himself, He embodied the full weight of human sin from the beginning of time.

“Maryam,” the heavenly voice thundered once more, “Accept your calling.”

With trembling hands and humble surrender, she reached out and received the Burden of the world.

And darkness closed around her, swallowing her whole.

When consciousness returned, she was standing in a city, empty, lifeless, as though all its inhabitants had vanished in a single instant. An autumn wind chased leaves through deserted streets, weaving strange, silent spirals.

Suddenly, the ground shook beneath her feet.

A trumpet blast rang out, so powerful that it was heard in all four corners of the earth.

And in the sky, a Sign appeared, driving away the darkness.

The light grew brighter and brighter until it filled the entire world.

Then the impossible happened.

Shadows appeared beyond the horizon.

First one.

Then another.

Then a third.

They took on flesh again.

They became people.

The city came back to life.

"You did it," a familiar voice said softly.

"Your sacrifice gave them a chance."

Maryam looked around. People were returning. The city was breathing again, filled with sound, movement, life.

But she felt it: her time was slipping away.

Her body grew light. Her breath barely lingered.

She lifted her eyes to the radiant sky.

The light was blinding—yet there was no pain in it. Only infinite peace, and the tenderness with which one is welcomed home after fulfilling their calling.

"Glory be to You, Lord..." she whispered.

And she stepped into the Light.

ABOUT THE AUTHOR

The author is a mother of four and a contemporary writer whose work is deeply infused with spiritual inquiry and reflections on humanity's destiny. In her debut novel, she turns to timeless themes, the struggle between good and evil, faith and unbelief, revealing them through the prism of her characters' personal journeys.

A person of broad intellectual horizons, the author studies various religious traditions and philosophical teachings, which are vividly reflected in her writing. Her profound interest in the spiritual realm has enabled her to create a multilayered world in which human destinies intertwine with higher powers.

At the heart of her first novel lies not only artistic imagination but also a deep engagement with apocalyptic themes, religious prophecy, and philosophical concepts. The author seeks to show that even in the darkest of times, the human soul can find a path toward the Light.

The novel gives particular attention to the themes of motherhood and the protection of children's spiritual values—an area the author considers one of the most vital issues of the modern world. Through the protagonist's image, she reveals the power of maternal love as one of the most fundamental spiritual forces.

Explosion is not merely a work of fiction; it is a parable-novel—a profound meditation on the future of humanity, the role of spirituality in the contemporary world, and the challenge of preserving humaneness amid global catastrophe. The author invites the reader to reflect on eternal questions and to seek answers together.

Made in the USA
Monee, IL
16 May 2026

74b30636-259e-4d21-a4c0-280aa7fa867fR01